the world's GREATEST underachiever

HankZipZER

THE LiFE OF ME
(ENTER AT YOUR OWN RISK)

HENRY WiNKLER & LiN OLiUER

WALKER
ENTERTAINMENT

First published in Great Britain 2014 by Walker Books Ltd
87 Vauxhall Walk, London SE11 5HJ

First published in the United States as *Hank Zipzer #14: The Life of Me (Enter at Your Own Risk)* (2008) by Henry Winkler and Lin Oliver. Published by arrangement with Grosset & Dunlap™, a division of Penguin Young Readers Group, a member of Penguin Group (USA) Inc. All rights reserved.

2 4 6 8 10 9 7 5 3 1

This book has been typeset in Sabon

Printed and bound in Great Britain by Clays Ltd, St Ives plc

British Library Cataloguing in Publication Data:
a catalogue record for this book is available from the British Library

ISBN 978-1-4063-5577-2

www.walker.co.uk

This book is dedicated to a gift of a partner,
who happens to be very gifted,
and to Stacey, as always. – H.W.

For Steve Mooser – my wonderful partner
since way back under the fig tree. – L.O.

CHAPTER 1

"SO I'M IN MY BEST martial arts crouch, ready to let loose a whopper roundhouse kick," I said to my best friend Frankie Townsend as we waited for the red light to change at the corner of 78th and Amsterdam. "And Nick McKelty is right in front of me, pressed up against a brick wall, begging for mercy and whining like a baby."

"You had that big-mouth bully cornered?" Frankie said. "No way, Zip."

"He was all mine," I said proudly.

"And then what happened?" Ashley Wong, my other best friend, asked. She was so totally engrossed in my story that she didn't even notice that the light had turned green.

"Suddenly, McKelty breaks free. He stops whining and springs at me, flashing his teeth like an angry lion."

"So what'd you do?" Frankie asked.

"I let out a loud whoop, spun around like

a top and landed that roundhouse kick on his squishy butt. I think my footprint made a permanent impression on his rear end."

Frankie and Ashley laughed out loud.

"Way to go, Zip," Frankie said. "You're the man."

"Oh, you know I am," I said. "That McKelty went down as hard as Swampman when the Lagoon Creature gave it to him between the eyes."

"Wow, Hank," Ashley said as we stepped off the kerb and headed across the street. "When did this fight happen?"

"Last night."

Frankie squinted his eyes and gave me a funny look.

"Dude, I was with you last night until bedtime," he said. "Remember, we were quizzing each other on spelling words."

"Sure, I remember."

"So, Hank, exactly when last night did you have this battle with McKelty?" Ashley asked.

"In my dreams," I said. "Ashweena, I was all-powerful. When I landed that kick, he couldn't even see it coming. My foot was faster than the speed of light."

"For a minute there, Zip, you had me believing this actually happened," Frankie said.

"It did actually happen. It just happened in my dreams."

"I love dreams," Ashley said. "Last night, I dreamed I shared a peanut butter and jam sandwich with a dolphin."

"And they say girls don't know how to have fun," I said. Frankie and I cracked up and Ashley shot us a dirty look.

"I know why you had that dream," Frankie said as we trudged up the last half a block to our school.

"Me too," Ashley chimed in. "It's because Nick McKelty is a bragging, obnoxious bully who needs to be put in his place."

"No," Frankie said. "I mean yes, but no. Yes and no."

"Is it just me or is Frankie making no sense at all?" Ashley said with a laugh.

Frankie stopped walking and looked at us both. "OK, here's what I mean," he said. "Yes, McKelty is a world-famous jerk. But no, Zip's dream isn't about McKelty. It's about Zip. He's mentally preparing himself for our Tae Kwon Do class."

Feeling that he had cleared everything up, Frankie started walking again. As I hurried to catch up with him, I thought about what he had said. True, we were starting our once-a-week after-school Tae Kwon Do class that day. And true, I was really looking forward to it. And true, it would feel great to be the best one in the class. And true, even though I would probably never do it, I would love to know that I could take down McKelty, even if it was only in my dreams.

Wow, I wonder how my brain figured all that out when I was asleep and put it into such a cool dream? Way to go, brain!

"Hey, Hankster," Frankie said when Ashley and I were once again by his side. "Remember when we took karate in pre-school? You were a little champ. I bet you're going to be the master of our Tae Kwon Do after-school class. Except for me, of course."

"We'll be co-masters," I said, knowing that Frankie Townsend was an ace athlete and way better at everything than I was. If I turned out to be half as good as him in Tae Kwon Do, I'd be happy.

"Did you remember to get your parents to sign your permission slip?" Ashley asked me.

"They won't let you start without it."

"Who do you think I am, Forgetto-Man?" I laughed. "It's right here."

I jammed my hand into my jeans pocket to show Ashley that, of course, I had the signed permission slip. OK, so it wasn't in that pocket. I checked the other front pocket. Oops, not there, either. I didn't panic, because we all know that jeans have a lot of pockets. I just calmly shoved both my hands in my back pockets, and they both found out together that it wasn't there, either.

Hank to permission slip? Where are you? Show yourself.

"Zip, you didn't forget it again?" Frankie shook his head at me.

I have to say that I was a teensy bit worried. I really, really, really wanted to do the after-school Tae Kwon Do class. And I really, really, really wasn't finding the permission slip.

"I know that I picked it up from my desk this morning," I said, retracing my steps in my mind. "Then I walked with it into the kitchen, put it next to my oatmeal at breakfast, picked it up again when I was finished, walked into the bathroom to brush my teeth, got a little toothpaste on it, rubbed that off, left the bathroom and walked to the front door, and put it … put it … into my rucksack!"

"Phew!" Ashley said. "I thought we were never going to get there."

"Pull the zip, Frankie," I said as I turned around so my rucksack was facing him. "See if it's in there."

Frankie pulled the zip, reached into the pouch and came up with two pencils with the rubbers bitten off, one ball, and then … ta-da … my permission slip.

"Ladies and gentlemen, I give you the long-lost Zipzer Permission Slip," he said.

We didn't even have a second to celebrate, because the final bell was ringing as we reached the grey cement steps of our school. Mr Love, who is not only the head teacher of our school, but also the owner of the world's largest collection of snowman scarves, was holding the door open.

"Welcome to the halls of learning, children," he said to us, adjusting his red scarf so we'd get a clear view of the tap-dancing snowmen wearing black top hats. You could tell he was really proud of that scarf.

"Hello, Mr Love," Ashley said. "Nice scarf."

Frankie and I shot her a look. I mean, just because the guy wears a snowman scarf every day doesn't mean you have to encourage him to do it.

"Wait until you see the one I'm wearing tomorrow," Mr Love said. "I don't want to ruin the surprise, but I will tell you it involves snowmen on seesaws."

Fortunately for us, we were already late and had to hurry upstairs to class, so there wasn't time to come up with something to say. I think you'll agree that snowmen on seesaws aren't exactly an easy topic of conversation.

"Enter quickly," Mr Love said, waving us through the door. "And allow your minds to open to the ideas that fill the open mind, as open as this door is that I hold open for you."

If you're trying to figure out what Mr Love actually meant, please do not weary your brains any longer. No one at our school has ever understood anything that he has to say, at least not for the six years and four months that I've been a student here. You just kind of smile at him and nod. A lot.

So we all did a lot of nodding, then shot up to class. Ms Adolf, our teacher, does not appreciate tardiness. She's told us that once or twice. Or ninety times. No tardiness is only one of her rules. A few of her others are: No Laughing, No Smiling, No Grinning, No Happy Movement of the Lips at All. Aside from the Nos, there are her "dislikes". A few of those include misspelled words, any colour other than grey, nicknames and odd smells that come from either your lunch or your body. Oh, I forgot her biggest dislike. Children.

Ms Adolf sure makes fifth grade fun. Don't you wish you had her, too?

We bolted into class and slammed on the brakes immediately, because one of the Big Nos that I forgot to mention is No Running in Class.

I didn't even look up as I slowly slunk to my chair. I guess I thought if I moved slowly enough, I'd be invisible and she wouldn't mention that I had arrived after the bell rang. So you can imagine my surprise when I heard a man's voice say, "Good morning, you guys," which, by the way, was not followed by, "Take out your lined paper and get ready for a pop quiz." That – and the manly voice – were definite tip-offs that it was not Ms Adolf speaking.

I looked up, and to my surprise, standing

14

before us was Mr Rock. He's the music teacher, and by the way, the coolest teacher in the whole school. He's a pal of mine. Mr Rock was the one who convinced my parents to have me tested to see if I had learning difficulties, which, by the way, I do. Ever since then, Mr Rock and I have had a special connection. He really understands that my brain has a mind of its own.

"Hey, Mr Rock, how are you doing?" I shouted out before I could lasso my tongue to stop it from talking out loud. My tongue and I seem to have a problem with impulse control. But Mr Rock didn't even mind that I hadn't raised my hand. And how did I know that? Because here's what he said:

"Great to see you, Hank. How's tricks?"

Imagine *that* coming out of Ms Adolf's mouth! It never would. What would come out of her mouth was, "In my classroom, pupils raise their hands before speaking."

"Everything's fine, Mr Rock," I answered. "Not to be rude, but what are you doing here?"

"Well, funny you should ask, Hank. Because I was just about to tell the class that you guys have the good fortune to have me as your long-term substitute teacher for the next four weeks."

Four weeks of Mr Rock! My ears started jumping for joy. The words weren't even out of his mouth when the whole class burst into applause.

"Unfortunately," Mr Rock went on, trying to ignore the applause, "your teacher, Ms Adolf, has thrown out her back while participating in one of her favourite hobbies."

My hands were applauding, my ears were jumping for joy, but my mind went into list-making overdrive. What possible hobby could Ms Adolf have that would cause her to throw out her back?

CHAPTER 2

TEN WAYS MS ADOLF COULD
HAVE THROWN HER BACK OUT
WHILE PARTICIPATING IN HER
FAVOURITE HOBBY

1. Maybe she was a contestant in the Strongest Woman in the World competition and was towing a jumbo jet down the runway by a rope tied around only her left ankle.
2. Maybe while scuba diving she was attacked by a giant squid, which mistook her for a spiny crab (which, by the way, she is).
3. Maybe once the squid realized that she wasn't a spiny crab, he used three of his eight arms as a slingshot to fling her back to shore, where she landed on her back. Ouch.
4. Maybe she was bowling, and her fingers got stuck in the ball, and she threw herself

down the lane. (*Hank's note*: If you knock all the pins down with your body and not the ball, I wonder if that's still considered a strike?)

5. Maybe she's a rodeo rider and a bucking bronco bucked her off so hard that she went into orbit and landed on her back in New Jersey.

6. Maybe she was in a spelling bee and got so upset when she misspelled "receive" (like I always do) that she fainted and fell off the stage and landed on the world's biggest dictionary.

7. Maybe she was writing a Big Fat Red D on my last maths test with such force that her whole back went into a spasm and all of a sudden half of her was facing frontwards and the other half was facing backwards.

8. Maybe she has a secret life as a ballroom dancer and was injured while doing a wild rumba turn with her handsome partner from Argentina. No, what are you thinking, Hank? That's way too cool a thing for Ms Adolf to ever do.

9. ...

My list came to an abrupt stop when I suddenly heard my name being spoken by Mr Rock.

"Hank ... Hank..."

CHAPTER 3

"... HANK, AS I WAS SAYING, Ms Adolf was injured while doing a triple turn in a rumba contest with her partner from Argentina," Mr Rock said.

No way.

She really is that cool!

Hank Zipzer, you're a psychic!

I mean, a guy doesn't just randomly think that his teacher is a rumba dancer and then it turns out to be true, unless he has powers from the great beyond. Maybe I should open a fortune-telling office. And get a turban. I don't need a crystal ball; I've got one in my brain. I immediately got busy imagining what my business cards would look like. Should they be simple and just say, "Hank Zipzer, Mind Reader"? Or maybe I should go with something rhyming like, "Hank the Fortune Teller for Gals and Fellers." Or maybe something weird and mysterious like, "Travel with Swami Zipzer to the Great Beyond."

I was still trying to decide if my cards should be blue with white letters or black with orange letters and a purple lightning bolt when I thought I heard my name mentioned again.

"Were you listening, Hank?" Mr Rock was saying when I checked back into reality.

"Um … does half-listening count?" I asked him. "Because I heard a lot of what you said, just not the last part."

"You mean the part where I asked everyone to open their history books to chapter seven?" Mr Rock said with a smile.

"Those words just whizzed by my head at supersonic speed, Sir," I said.

Everyone cracked up, everyone except Nick McKelty. Nick McKelty only laughs at things he says or does. And by the way, the things he does are never funny … unless you consider sticking your tongue out to show people a half-eaten granola bar funny. That's his idea of a major laugh.

I quickly opened my book. I didn't want to be a flake when Mr Rock was teaching. He was being really nice about my not listening. Ms Adolf would have given me a big-time lecture about the importance of paying attention. I flipped through the pages, but I wasn't finding chapter seven.

McKelty reached over to my desk and turned to the right page.

"Here you go, Zipperbutt. Chapter seven. I found it because I knew you couldn't."

"That's enough of that talk, Nick," Mr Rock said. "Now, let's begin by reading the chapter introduction out loud. And by the way, guys, if you're wondering why we're doing this, it's because I teach music and not American government, and this chapter is about American government. So we're all going to learn together. OK?"

I told you Mr Rock was cool. I mean, when was the last time you heard a teacher admit that he didn't know that much about the subject so you're all going to learn together?

"Let's start with Ashley in row one," Mr Rock said. "We'll go around the room and each person will come to the front and read a paragraph. That sounds pretty painless, doesn't it?"

That was when my brain pushed the panic button. It's not that I have anything against history. I actually loved it when we learned about the ancient Egyptians and how they buried their kings with gold jewellery and lots of food and stuff so they would be happy and not too hungry in the afterlife. But if there's one thing on this whole earth that is unbelievably hard for me, it's reading out loud. I stumble over words, even simple ones that I know how to read. My eyes jump around on the page so much that I can't follow even a single sentence. I see words that aren't there, and leave out the ones that are. It's really frustrating for me, because I feel like I could read out loud with great expression, if I could just get the words right.

"Bet you can't wait for your turn. Right, Zipper Dunce?" McKelty whispered.

McKelty's been listening to me screw up reading out loud since first grade, and he really enjoys giving me a hard time about it. I knew he was looking forward to watching me get up in front of the class and make a fool of myself.

Ashley read the first paragraph, and she was perfect, as always. It was all about how the Founding Fathers set up the Constitution and the government and all that stuff. The only thing I kept thinking was why the Founding Fathers had to use so many big words that were hard to pronounce.

After Ashley, we went across the front row. Katie Sperling and Ryan Shimozato and Heather Payne all read. After each paragraph, we would stop and Mr Rock would talk about what was interesting or important. I kept raising my hand and asking a lot of questions, hoping that we'd use up all the history time before we got to my turn to read.

"How come they were called Founding Fathers and not Founding Dads?" I asked.

"Why did they call it a Constitution and not A Bunch of Rules?"

"When the Founding Fathers met in Philadelphia, did they eat a cheesesteak? And if they did, was it with or without the cheese sauce?"

"I didn't know you were so fascinated by American history," Mr Rock said to me after my third question. "I'm glad to see that, Hank."

But even with all my questions, the old hands on the clock were moving slowly and there was still time for more reading. That meant we moved into the next row. My row.

Frankie went next, then Nick McKelty, who was lucky and got the shortest paragraph on the page. It was only one sentence long. Why couldn't that have been me?

I guess McKelty got through his reading OK, but I really wouldn't know because I didn't hear a word he read. All I heard was the thumping of my heart. It gets really loud when I get nervous, and I was big-time nervous.

"OK, Hank," Mr Rock said. "The next paragraph is yours. Come on up."

"Mr Rock," I said, "I would love to do some oral reading, really I would. But it's just that I woke up this morning with a frog in my throat. Didn't I, Frankie?"

Frankie gave me one of those "Are you nuts, dude?" looks. I shot him back one of my "If I ever needed you, it's now, dude" looks. And without missing a beat, Frankie came through.

"He sounded so hoarse, he must have swallowed a bullfrog," Frankie said. "Isn't that right, Ashley?"

Ashley gave him one of her "Oh, don't drag me into this" looks, and I shot her one my "Hey, what are friends for?" looks. And without missing a beat, Ashley came through.

"It was such a big bullfrog, we almost saddled him up and rode him to school," she said.

Now the whole class was rolling in the aisles

and stomping their feet. Mr Rock laughed too.

"You're a lot of fun, Hank," he said.

I grinned and sighed with relief. Wow, that had been a close call, but once again, my sense of humour had got me out of an embarrassing situation.

Oops, not so fast, Hank.

"But," Mr Rock went on, "I don't hear you being hoarse now, so it seems that the bullfrog has moved to another pond. Come on up and don't forget your book."

I didn't understand why Mr Rock was making me do this. He must have known that I'd hate it.

The walk to the front of the class seemed like it was seven thousand miles long. My feet felt like they had hundred-pound weights attached to them. My stomach was flipping and flopping all over the place. This was really my worst nightmare.

I opened the book and cleared my throat.

CHAPTER 4

BEFORE I BEGAN, I took another look at the clock.

"It's getting late," I pointed out to Mr Rock.

"Late for what, Hank?"

"Um ... maths," I answered. "You want to be sure to save enough time for maths."

Was this me, wanting to do maths? Yes, it was, which told me how desperate I was. Anything was better than reading out loud. Even long division.

"Thanks, Hank," Mr Rock said. "But I think we're all finding the story of how our government was formed really interesting. Am I right, guys?"

Everyone in the class nodded, even Luke Whitman, which is really something, because it's not easy to nod with your finger in your nose without poking yourself really hard.

"So go ahead, Hank. Everybody follow along as he reads," Mr Rock said.

"You're not going to want to do that," I

mumbled under my breath. I mean, where were they going to follow me? Into the confused mess that is my brain? Once they get in there, they'll never get out.

"Mr Rock," I said. "I just remembered that I never got my flu shot this year, so I'll read as soon as I get back from the nurse's office."

I turned to go.

"Hank," Mr Rock said. "I know this isn't your favourite thing to do. But it's important to practise your reading. We're all here to learn, and learning takes practice. So give it a try. If you need help, I'll help you. Take your time. We've got time, don't we, kids?"

"This is going to take Mr Stupid until next year," McKelty shouted out.

"There'll be none of that, Nick," Mr Rock said. "We are a supportive learning community in this class. You don't make progress unless you try. So now, Hank, go ahead."

I took a breath and looked down at the page.

"Chapter seven," I said, even though everyone knew we were reading chapter seven. I just wanted to get off to a good start. I wasn't even reading the words, I was remembering them.

"The Founding Fathers divided the American

government into three branches," I read.

"That's excellent, Hank," Mr Rock said.

Wow. So far, so good. This wasn't so hard.

"They are called the..."

I stopped dead in my tracks, because three of the longest, hardest words you have ever seen popped out of nowhere. These weren't branches of government, they were alphabet traps. Why did they have to call them *that*, whatever *that* was? I mean, what's wrong with olive branch, pine branch and maple branch? At least I had a shot at reading those.

No, this branch was the ... whatever it was, it started with an *L*.

"Just try to sound out the word," Mr Rock said. "Break the word down into syllables."

"Mr Rock, I think I've gone about as far as I can go," I said. "Can't we call it the 'L' branch and let me sit down?"

"Yeah," McKelty called out. "Let Zipperbutt sit down. He's a lost cause."

"Nick, that's enough from you," Mr Rock said, with real impatience in his voice now. "We show one another respect in this classroom. Just because each of us learns differently, it doesn't mean we all don't have greatness in us."

I didn't know what to feel. On the one hand, having Mr Rock stick up for me felt great. And I was proud that I had started out pretty good. On the other hand, not being able to read out loud is totally, completely embarrassing. You try feeling embarrassed and proud at the same time. It's very confusing.

"That's a good beginning, Hank," Mr Rock said. "You happened to get a very difficult paragraph, and you gave it a good shot."

Mr Rock didn't insist that I go on, so I hurried to my seat faster than you could say Founding Fathers. After me, three more people read about the branches of government. I should point out two things here. Number one: None of them had any trouble at all reading the names of the three branches of government or any other word on the page. And number two: I now know that the three branches of government are the legislative, executive and judicial branches. When you think about it, that makes a whole lot more sense than the olive, pine and maple branches.

The minute the bell rang for break, I slammed my book shut and bolted for the door. Before I could make it into the hallway, Mr Rock asked if he could see me for a minute. He waited until the class was empty, then perched himself on the edge of Ms Adolf's desk, swinging a leg as he talked to me. I noticed that he had green frogs all over his blue socks. I like it when adults wear funny animals somewhere on their clothes. It's like saying, "I'm an adult, but not all the way through."

"So, Hank," he began. "Seems like reading is still pretty challenging for you."

"Only some words," I said. "I'm a whizz at 'and,' 'cat,' and 'the'."

He laughed and then stopped laughing.

"Seriously, Hank, would you like to be better at reading?"

"Seriously, sure I would. It's not fun to stand in front of the class and not be able to get two words out. But maybe McKelty is right. Maybe I am a lost cause and I just have to learn to live with it."

"No, you don't," Mr Rock said, putting a hand on my shoulder. "In fact, the school is starting a new programme called the Reading Gym, which is intended for students just like you."

"The Reading Gym?" I said. "What do you do, hang from a trapeze and read upside down?"

"We practise reading, just like a gymnast practises tumbling or trampolining."

"Maybe I'll come sometime," I said. "It sounds OK."

"I'd like you to come after school this afternoon," Mr Rock said. "I'm the Reading Gym teacher, and if we work together, I think your reading skills could go through the roof."

"Sorry, Mr Rock, but I'm doing the Tae Kwon Do after-school programme, which is starting today also."

"Maybe I could call your mum and dad and discuss the possibility of you switching to the Reading Gym," Mr Rock said. "I could explain to them why I think you need it and could benefit from it."

"No!" I said, maybe even a little too quickly. "Don't do that!"

The last thing I wanted was my dad getting another call from school saying that I needed special help. His theory about me, even though he knows I have learning difficulties, is that if I concentrate and work really hard and, as he says, "keep my bottom in the chair and study", I'll do fine in school. He is definitely not a big fan of the call from the teacher saying I'm behind in reading or behind in maths or just behind in anything.

"OK, Hank," Mr Rock said. "Let's keep this conversation between us for now. But think this over. I'd like you to seriously consider participating in the Reading Gym. It will give you skills that will help you for the rest of your life."

"I'll think about it," I said.

"I know you'll make the right decision, Hank," Mr Rock answered. "Now go to break. You've earned it."

I bolted out of the door, knowing full well what my decision was going to be. I mean, give me a break. If you had to choose between learning how to do a really cool roundhouse kick and learning how to sound out short vowel sounds, what would you choose?

It wasn't even close.

CHAPTER 5

OK, I CONFESS. I did feel kind of guilty as I walked into the gym for the after-school Tae Kwon Do class. A little voice inside was telling me that improving my reading was probably more important than learning to punch a board in half with my bare hands. Oddly enough, that little voice sounded a lot like my dad's.

But all that guilt went away when I caught my reflection in the gym window. We had all been given a new white gi, which is the traditional uniform of the martial artist. And as I caught a glimpse of myself in my gi, I thought to myself, *Wow, do I look powerful.* Hey, you know I'm not stuck-up and I wasn't just standing there admiring myself. But the thought did cross my mind that I was going to be good at martial arts.

I didn't get to enjoy that thought for very long, because joining me in my reflection was a gigantic blob of white that looked like a bag of marshmallows that had melted together. It was Nick McKelty in a gi the size of the Goodyear Blimp.

"What are you doing, Zipperbutt?" he said. "Posing for animal crackers?"

"Yeah, I was thinking about being the lion," I said. "Wanna hear me roar?" Then I growled in his face and walked away.

OK, so it was babyish, but it felt really good.

I turned around to see Frankie and Ashley watching me, laughing their heads off.

"That deserves a three-way high five," Frankie said. And we all put up our palms and slapped one another five.

Suddenly, the loudspeaker in the gym buzzed and a large, deep voice came blaring out.

"Attention, young masters in the making," the voice said. "Your sensei approaches."

There were ten or eleven other kids in the Tae Kwon Do class, and we all stopped what we were doing and turned our attention to the door. We waited and watched. Joelle Atkins, who has the icky pleasure of being Nick McKelty's girlfriend, actually got off her mobile phone, which is something that only happens every eighty years like one of those weird comets that flies by. Katie Sperling stopped messing with the scrunchie that holds back her blonde ponytail and stood to attention. Ashley pushed her purple glasses back on her nose and craned her neck to see if she could see anyone coming. I have to confess, even I edged my way to the front of the group so I could get the first look. We could hardly wait to meet our teacher, the sensei who would teach us how to throw punches and land kicks. Then we heard footsteps coming down the hall. They were squeaky.

Wait a minute, I thought to myself. *I'm positive I know that squeak.*

"There's only one person whose shoes squeak like that!" I whispered to Ashley.

But before she could answer, our sensei appeared in the doorway. He was none other than Head Teacher Leland Love, wearing his favourite goofy Velcro sneakers that squeaked wherever he went. I don't even want to tell you what he was wearing above the sneakers. OK, I will, but you're not going to believe it. He was wearing a gi with short trousers that looked like Bermuda shorts. Below them, you could see his pale legs, wrinkly black socks and, of course, the brown imitation leather Velcro sneakers. And wrapped around his waist was the scarf with the tap-dancing snowmen. It wasn't a pretty sight.

"Young masters, I am your sensei," Mr Love said. "Your teacher, trainer and inspirational leader."

There was a buzz that went around the group. I didn't want to turn around and stare, so I couldn't tell exactly who was saying what, but my ears picked up the following.

"You've got to be kidding."

"What's he know about this?"

"I thought this was going to be fun."

"That's the biggest gi I've ever seen."

"I'm calling my mum to come and get me."

As for me, I just kept looking at Mr Love's knees. It's hard to take someone seriously as your inspirational leader if their knobby knees are staring you in the face.

"What's with the short trousers?" I whispered to Frankie. "Doesn't that seem strange?"

"Maybe he left his gi in the dryer too long and it shrank," Frankie said.

"That makes sense," Ashley said. "Because no one would go after that look on purpose."

"Except a turtle," I said. "It looks like his arms and legs are coming out of a shell."

We had to cover our mouths and turn away from Mr Love to keep from laughing. But when we couldn't hold it in any more, a couple of smushed-down laughs leaked out of our covered lips. Mr Love shot all three of us a stern look.

"The martial arts are no laughing matter," he said. "What exactly are you finding so funny, Mr Zipzer?"

"Um ... I was just thinking about a really funny turtle joke," I said. "Would you like to hear it?"

Ashley poked me in the ribs with her elbow so hard I thought she was trying to crack one. There was a look of horror on her face as if to say, "You're not really going to tell him what we're thinking, are you?"

"Why, yes, Hank. I would," Mr Love said. "Why don't you share it with us all?"

Frankie was shaking his head no, as he inched away from me. I'm sure he was terrified that I was going to say something about how Mr Love looked like a turtle coming out of its shell.

But as much as I can't remember how to spell almost any word, I happen to have a great memory for jokes, and I had a turtle one ready to go on the tip of my tongue.

"Why did the turtle cross the road?" I said.

"I'm sure I wouldn't know," Mr Love answered.

"To get to the Shell station."

To my amazement, Mr Love threw his head back with such force that what little hair he had surrounding his bald spot flew into the air. Then he let out a huge laugh. And kept laughing for a really long time. Man, that guy must have been really starved for jokes. I mean, the turtle joke is cute, but it's not a throw-your-bald-head-back-and-scream kind of joke.

Mr Love has this mole on his cheek that is shaped like the Statue of Liberty without the torch. Well, let me tell you, his mole looked like it was doing the hula as he laughed his head off. I watched it jiggle on his face, and my mind pictured that mole in a gi with a green belt holding the jacket closed. I cracked up again.

"Thank you, Mr Zipzer, for that moment of levity," Mr Love said. "And what are you finding so humorous now? Another joke, perhaps?"

I really couldn't tell him this time. I mean,

whose brain imagines a facial mole dressed in a martial arts outfit? Only mine, I'm sure.

"That turtle just keeps cracking me up, Sir," I said.

But by this time, Mr Love was over his laugh attack and ready to continue with the class.

"Let me begin by answering the question that I'm sure is on everyone's mind," he said, pacing back and forth in his gi shorts. "And that question must be, why is your esteemed head teaching a class on martial arts?"

Joelle Atkins's hand shot into the air.

"That wasn't the question on my mind," she said. "My question is, where can I keep my mobile phone during class? I love it more than anything and I don't want anyone else to touch it."

Ashley rolled her eyes back in her head so far I thought they were going to slip around the back and never come down.

"What's with her?" she whispered. "What kind of person is in love with a telephone?"

"I had a question on my mind," Jonah Pattison said. He is a big fifth-grader who seems to have a sweating problem. At least, he's always wearing a pretty sweaty looking sweatband around his curly hair, even in winter. It's weird, because he always wears a big jacket, too. If I were him, I'd take off the jacket, then maybe I wouldn't sweat so much and I could take off the sweatband, too. But that's me.

"What works better under this gi?" Jonah asked. "Boxers or briefs?"

"Eeuuuwww," said Katie Sperling, who was standing in between Jonah and Nick McKelty. "Nobody wants to discuss your underpants, Jonah."

Nick McKelty let out one of his monster laughs, spraying a few drops of saliva in the direction of Katie.

"Underpants," he howled. "That's a riot!"

Katie Sperling ducked to avoid his spit spray, then turned to Mr Love.

"May I please change places with Salvatore?" she said. Salvatore was standing at the total opposite side of the gym from Jonah and McKelty.

"Oh no, I'm not standing next to them," Salvatore said. "I don't want to be stuck between Sweaty and Spitty."

"Enough of this talk," Mr Love said, clapping his hands to get our attention. "I intend to answer the question I posed. Why am I teaching

41

the martial arts? Because, youngsters, what you don't know about me is that I am an expert practitioner of several martial arts. Underneath this head teacher's body beats the heart of a warrior."

Wow. My grandpa, Papa Pete, always says you can't judge a book by its cover, and boy, in this case, was he ever right. I mean, when you look at Mr Love, you're definitely not thinking Bruce Lee or Jackie Chan. I mean, can you see one of those guys in a snowman scarf? Or Velcro sneakers? I don't think so.

"Now gather around me, youngsters," Mr Love said, "and listen very carefully. We are here to summon our physical, spiritual and emotional energy to develop a strong moral character."

"Excuse me, Mr Love," I said, raising my hand to get his attention. "I think I'm in the wrong class. I thought we were going to learn how to break a piece of plywood with our foreheads."

"It is that kind of concentration that we are looking to develop in studying the martial arts," Mr Love said. "It will take time, focus, determination..."

"And a strong forehead," Jonah Pattison chimed in. "Which I'm not sure I have."

"You've got protection in that sweatband," Frankie said. "We've been waiting for that thing to come in handy for years."

Ashley laughed so hard that if she had been drinking milk, it would have come shooting out of her nose. Katie Sperling laughed too, and I noticed that she sent a really deluxe smile Frankie's way. And he returned it with his best dimple smile.

The very next second Katie Sperling changed places again and wiggled her way in between me and Frankie. Frankie is good at everything, and it was clear that Katie Sperling thought so too.

From the corner of my eye, I noticed some commotion in the hall outside the gym. It was Mr Rock herding about seven or eight kids into the library. They were making a lot of noise as they went in. Actually, it was more than noise. It was laughter, as in the sound you make when you're having a good time. That didn't make any sense. I mean, how could kids who were heading into the Reading Gym possibly be having a good time? And so soon?

"I'd like you all to go to your rucksacks and pull out a pencil and some paper as quickly and as quietly as possible," Mr Love said to us.

"Hey, I thought this was a fighting class," Nick McKelty called out. "Not a write-stuff-down class."

"If you are to be a practitioner of the ancient art of Tae Kwon Do, you must know its history," Mr Love said. "First we train the mind, then we train the body."

As I got a pencil and some paper out of my rucksack, I glanced out of the door and saw Mr Rock closing the door to the library across the hall. He caught my eye and waved.

"Come on over if you change your mind," he called out.

I scurried back to the circle and joined the other kids sitting on the gym floor. Mr Love started to pace back and forth in front of us, his Velcro shoes squeaking with each step.

"The earliest records show that Tae Kwon Do has been practised in Korea for over two thousand years," he began.

"Two thousand years!" I whispered to Frankie and Ashley. "We'll be taking notes until my next birthday."

"That's eleven months away," Ashley said.

"I don't have enough lead in my pencil for that!" I answered.

"Mr Zipzer," Mr Love said. "I'd like to see you whispering less and taking notes more. My lecture will be filled with fascinating details, such as a thorough and complete description of early cave paintings found on the ceiling of the Mu Yong-Chong tombs of people using techniques similar to modern Tae Kwon Do."

Was he kidding? Were we all dressed in gis so we could sit in the stuffy gym and take notes on a bunch of ancient guys painting on tomb ceilings? Where was the action? Where were the roundhouse kicks? Where was the fun?

Oh, I know. It probably listened for two seconds to Mr Love drone on about the history of Tae Kwon Do and said to itself, "I'm out of here," and ran as fast as it could out of the gym door.

And speaking of fun, from the sound of things, I'm pretty sure it ended up in Mr Rock's Reading Gym across the hall.

I looked around, saw that no one was watching me and headed out. I think you know where I was going.

CHAPTER 6

TWO REASONS WHY I FOLLOWED
THE FUN INTO MR ROCK'S CLASS

1. Mr Love's right knee.*
2. Mr Love's left knee.*

Hank's Note to Reader: I don't mean to be disrespectful to anybody's knees, BUT I do have to say that Mr Love's knees were definitely unacceptable to my eyes. That was because of:

A. wobbly skin where there should have been kneecap.

B. a large amount of hair covering the wobbly skin.

C. a mysterious pinkish rash on the left one.

D. all of the above.

The correct answer is D.

CHAPTER 7

I POKED MY NOSE into the library, where Mr Rock was holding the Reading Gym. But since I needed to *see* what was going on, and not *smell* what was going on, sticking my nose in didn't do me much good. So I stuck my whole head in.

About seven or eight kids were sitting around a large square table. To be completely and totally honest with you, I didn't even see who all the kids were because my eyes locked on one of them as they have never locked before. My stomach started to jimble-jamble like when you think you might have the stomach flu but you're not sure. My mouth went dry like I was lost in the desert. And I wanted to move, but my feet felt like they each weighed a ton and I couldn't take a step.

I thought I heard Mr Rock calling my name, but his voice sounded like it was hundreds of miles away.

Meanwhile, my eyes hadn't blinked once

since my head entered the room. And here's the weirdest part. What they were staring at was a girl. Not a Mets play-off on TV. Not a video game. Not a Swampman cartoon marathon. But an actual girl.

Did you hear me folks? I said a *girl*.

Now why would I, Hank Zipzer, be staring at a girl? Because she was beautiful, that's why. I don't know if you would think she was beautiful, because she wasn't like regular, magazine beautiful. But to my own personal green eyes and frozen brain, she was really something.

I could only see half her face because she was wearing a hat. Not a baseball hat, but a real hat like my grandpa, Papa Pete, would wear with what he calls a business suit. But the half of her face that I saw had an eye that was so blue it looked like the chest of the bright blue parakeet named Leo that lived with our neighbour Mrs Fink until she became allergic to him and had to give him to her son, Franklin.

The girl with the blue eye was wearing a red T-shirt with braces holding up her checked trousers. She had a look, this girl, that said, "Talk to me, I'm interesting."

If I could just get my feet to take a step into

the room, maybe I could start that conversation. But my feet were not co-operating. They clung to the floor like tree frogs hanging onto the trunks of trees in the rain forest.

Hank to feet. Hank to eyes. Hank to ears. Hank to all of Hank. Could any of you come to life? You've been in this doorway for a long time now, looking mighty goofy.

Fortunately, Mr Rock came to my rescue. He walked up to me with a big, friendly smile.

"Well, Hank, I see you've made the decision to come halfway in," he said. "Do you want to complete that decision and come all the way in?"

"Most of me wants to," I said. "But my feet seem to be the hold-outs here. They have a mind of their own."

I saw all seven kids crack up, but I could only hear her laugh. She had turquoise braces on her teeth, and I noticed that they matched her eyes perfectly.

Hank to brain. Are you actually thinking these thoughts? What is going on?

"Well, let me help your feet get started," Mr Rock said, "and escort you to a chair."

The Angel of Empty Chairs must have been smiling down on me, because the only available

49

chair was right next to her. I broke free of Mr Rock's hand on my shoulder and bolted over to that chair like a cheetah. Before I could even say, "I'm so happy I have a reading problem," my butt was in the chair and settling in next to her. I glanced over at her and noticed something amazing. She had a set of drumsticks sticking out of her back pocket.

A blue-eyed, hat-wearing, learning-challenged drummer. Is that the girl of my dreams or what?

My heart almost stopped when I noticed she was turning round and looking at me. That could mean only one thing. I was going to have to talk to her. What would I say? And worse than that, she was looking right at me, close-up. Did I remember to use a napkin after lunch, or did I have chunks of tuna sandwich crusted on the side of my mouth? I started to reach up and do a tuna check, but stopped suddenly. What if I found something? What then? If I brushed it off, it would just fall down on the table and stare us both in the face. What would I say then?

Excuse me, beautiful girl, but I seem to have saved some of my sandwich. Are you hungry? Would you like a bite?

That's terrible, Hank. You can't say that!

50

Luckily, I was pulled away from this nightmare thought by the sound of someone talking to me.

It was her.

"I used to do martial arts," she said, looking at my gi. "I have an orange belt."

A blue-eyed, hat-wearing, learning-challenged, drumstick-carrying roundhouse kicker! This was just getting better and better.

"My name is Zoe," she said. "For your information, it means 'life' in Greek."

"Hi," I said. "My name is Hank. I have no idea what it means, but it rhymes with tank. Also stank."

Hank Zipzer! What are you saying? Stop it right now. Wad up a piece of paper and stuff it in your mouth and don't say another word until you get control of yourself!

I was too embarrassed to even look at her, but I heard her. And she was laughing. In a really nice way.

There it was. The old Zipzer attitude. And guess what, guys? It was working!

CHAPTER 8

"WELCOME, EVERYONE, to the first meeting of the Reading Gym," Mr Rock said as I settled into my chair and tried to concentrate on what he was saying.

By the way, concentration is never easy for me, but it was especially hard with Zoe the Wonderful sitting next to me. All my brain kept thinking about was how someone so cool could be in Reading Gym. I mean, let's face it. As much as they tried to make this sound like a fun after-school sports club, it was still a class for those of us who aren't exactly swift learners.

I wondered if she was wondering about me. Like, what's this guy doing in here? What's his problem? Is he failing fifth grade?

"First, I want to congratulate each of you on making the decision to attend the Reading Gym," Mr Rock went on. "Each and every one of you is an individual. You are all so different in your own ways, and at the same time, you all share one thing in common."

"Yeah, we're stupid," Luke Whitman said, taking his finger out of his nostril just long enough to shout out this insulting remark.

I hadn't even noticed that Luke Whitman was there and was picking his nose as always. This should tell you how much I was focused on Zoe. I mean, it's almost impossible not to notice Luke Whitman picking his nose. It's so gross you just have to stare at him, like when you skin your knee really badly and you just have to keep staring at the scab.

"No one in here is stupid in any sense of the word," Mr Rock said, handing Luke a Kleenex from the pop-up box he kept on a side table.

"I don't need those," Luke said.

"Trust me, you do," Mr Rock said. "And next time, I suggest you bring your own."

"That boy is so gross," Zoe whispered to me.

"You think that's gross," I whispered back. "Every day he uses a different finger to go digging. And the amazing thing is, he always finds something."

Zoe cracked up and that made me feel pretty good. Maybe I had learning challenges, but the

Zipzer attitude was in fine form.

"What you guys share," Mr Rock went on, "is that you all learn differently. And no matter how you learn, it has nothing to do with your intelligence. What we're going to be doing in here is working on giving you techniques that will help you learn in a style that's best for you."

"I like him," Zoe whispered to me.

"Mr Rock is the best," I whispered back.

Look at this. We're having a real conversation, Zoe and me. Just like that. No sweat. Just talking. Wow, this is really something.

Mr Rock spent the next few minutes describing what was going to happen in the Reading Gym. Each student was going to create a book that told the story of his or her life. We'd all have to write the book, illustrate the book and then read the book to the group. And while we were making our life-story books, each of us would be working on our own individual learning issues like reading, writing, spelling, following directions and so on.

Leave it to Mr Rock to come up with a really interesting assignment like that. For a minute, I actually thought it was too bad I was going back to Tae Kwon Do and not staying in Reading Gym for the whole ten weeks. It sounded like fun. Of course, not as much fun as breaking a board with your bare hands. Once Mr Love got through the history of Tae Kwon Do and got into the actual kicking and board-breaking part, the class was going to really rock.

"Now," Mr Rock said, "how about we go around the room and have each of you say what is most difficult for you in school. That will help me figure out an individual strategy to help you. Let's start at this end of the room. Hank, that's you."

Mr Rock. What are you thinking? Can't you see I'm working hard to impress Zoe? And you want me to confess that I can't read, can't spell, can't do maths and can't do well in anything at school except lunch?

"Well," I said, trying to flash the old Zipzer grin. "I'm just here because I was doing the Tae Kwon Do class in the gym and I was getting tired of looking at the head teacher's knees, so I thought I'd take a hike across the hall until we get to the fighting and punching and kicking stuff."

"Hank," Mr Rock said. "I see you're not ready to share your issues, and that's OK. Let's move on to the young lady sitting next to you. What is your name?"

"Zoe," she said. "I'm in the fifth grade, but I read at a third-grade level because I have tracking difficulties with my eyes."

Wow. She just said it all, right out there. She doesn't care who knows that she reads at a third-grade level. That girl is fearless.

"We can work on that," Mr Rock said. "Reading exercises will make your eye muscles stronger and help you track better."

He gave her a big grin, and she smiled back at him. I wanted to be part of this smile fest. I stuck my hand up and waved it around urgently.

"Mr Rock, can I go again?" I said. "I think I'm ready."

"Sure, Hank," he said. "I'm all ears."

"My name is Hank Zipzer, and I'm in the fifth grade too. I don't know what grade level I read at, but I can tell you it's just above kindergarten. And I stink at spelling, and you can add maths to that too. I could wrap it up by saying I have learning challenges."

Mr Rock gave me a big smile.

"Excellent, Hank," he said. "The first step in getting help is to acknowledge that you need help. There's a lot we can accomplish in the Reading Gym."

"Whoah there, Mr Rock," I said. "I'm not actually in the Reading Gym. I mean, I'm *in* the Reading Gym, but not actually *in* the Reading Gym, if you know what I mean."

Zoe giggled.

"It's complicated," I whispered to her.

"You can say that again," she said.

After me, we went around the room and the other kids said what their school problems were. At least, I think that's what they said. I have to admit that I was only half listening. The other half of me was watching Zoe. I noticed that she was a doodler, just like me. She spent the whole hour drawing lightning bolts all over the front of her notebook with a glittery purple pen. She was a leg shaker like me too. Her knee bounced up and down like it had a motor in it.

"Are you going to stay in Reading Gym for the whole ten weeks?" I whispered to her, just after a shy girl named Chelsea described how she had difficulty reading because she was dyslexic and reversed letters on the page.

"Sure," said Zoe. "But it sounds like you're not staying. Too bad. We could have fun."

Hold on, ears! Did you just hear what I heard? She thinks we could have fun. Oh yeah.

57

Hank and Zoe. Zoe and Hank. Having fun.

"Well, actually, I'm not exactly sure what I'm doing," I said. "I mean, I told my two best friends that I'd do martial arts."

"And they're counting on you?" Zoe asked.

"Well, they're kind of counting on me, but not actually counting on me. It's…"

"I know," Zoe said. "Complicated."

Wow, this girl really gets me. I mean, look, we're already talking like we've known each other our whole lives.

We listened for a minute while another kid, Brandon Clarke, explained his reading difficulties. When he had finished talking, I suddenly heard my mouth whispering something that my brain hadn't planned to say.

"You know what?" I whispered to Zoe. "I've decided to stay here. I think Reading Gym will be much more fun than some old martial arts class. And, besides, my friends have each other."

Was that me talking? The same me that had been looking forward to Tae Kwon Do for weeks? The me that couldn't wait to execute roundhouse kicks and leap in the air like a pouncing tiger? Hank Zipzer, have you lost your mind?

"I'm glad," Zoe said.

"You are?"

"Sure, it's nice that you want to improve."

"Improvement is my middle name," I said.

It is? the old me was saying to this new me. *I thought it was Daniel.*

"What's your last name?" She giggled.

"Zipzer," I said with a smile. "What's yours?"

"McKelty," she said.

The smile froze on my face like I had just swallowed an iceberg.

"McKelty? As in McKelty McKelty? Like Nick McKelty?"

"Yeah, he's my first cousin."

Oh no. This couldn't be true.

It was just my luck.

I finally meet the blue-eyed, hat-wearing, learning-challenged, drum-playing, roundhouse kicking girl of my dreams, and can you believe it, she's a ... I can barely even say it ... she's a McKelty!

CHAPTER 9

NINE WAYS ZOE MCKELTY IS NOT LIKE HER CREEPY COUSIN NICK

1. She does not have brown cookie crumbs stuffed in between her two front teeth and crusted around the corners of her mouth.
2. She does not call me Zipperbutt, Zipperhead or Zipper Doofus.
3. She does not go around saying that her father is best friends with everyone from the Queen of England to every guy in the Baseball Hall of Fame, even the dead guys.
4. She does not have a thick neck the size of one of those five-thousand-year-old redwood trees.
5. Her breath does not smell like burning rubber.
6. She does not lie about how she is the best at everything including things she has

never even done like pole-vaulting, bungee jumping and camel racing.

7. When she laughs, she does not sound like a woodpecker with a stomachache.
8. Oh yeah, and the main way she's not like Nick McKelty is this: She likes me.
9. There, I said it. She likes me!

CHAPTER 10

"ABSOLUTELY NO WAY, ZIP!" Frankie said to me as we walked home from school that day. "Tell me you have not developed a wild crush on a member of the McKelty family!"

"Listen to me, Frankie, she's not like him. There is nothing about Zoe that is anything like Nick."

"Well, I think it's sweet," Ashley said. "Hank's love is going to overcome the McKelty-Zipzer rivalry and turn Nick into a real sweetie pie."

I stopped dead in my tracks, right there in the middle of the crowd of people shoving their way along Amsterdam Avenue.

"Just a minute, Ashweena," I said. "Who said anything about love? All I said about Zoe was that she is beautiful, nice, interesting, kind, funny and totally awesome."

"Sounds like love to me," Ashley said with a laugh.

Unfortunately, just then, Papa Pete appeared about a half a block away, waving his newspaper in the air to get our attention.

"Hey, kids," he called out. "Wait up!"

Let me just say that the only unfortunate thing about Papa Pete's arrival was that it didn't give me time to answer Ashley and tell her that I was definitely *not* in love. Everything else about him showing up was great, for several reasons. One, Papa Pete is extremely cool and it is always fun to see him. And two, he almost always offers to buy us a slice of pizza at Harvey's, which is the best and cheesiest pizza in the whole world.

"Let me buy you kids a slice of pizza," Papa Pete said when he reached us. "I happen to know Harvey has a fresh pie coming out of the oven right about now."

What'd I tell you? That Papa Pete is the best.

We walked over to Broadway, went inside Harvey's and sat down on four stools at the counter. I ordered a slice with pepperoni, Frankie ordered meatballs and extra cheese, and Ashley ordered mushrooms and sausage. Papa Pete ordered a coffee and a doughnut.

"So how are my grandkids?" Papa Pete asked. Even though only one of us is officially his grandkid, he likes to include Frankie and Ashley in the family too.

"Did you hear the news?" Ashley said as Harvey brought her a paper plate with the steaming hot slice of mushroom-sausage pizza. "Hank is in love."

"No kidding," Papa Pete said, brushing a few doughnut crumbs off his furry black mustache.

"I am not!" I said.

"Who's the lucky girl?" Harvey asked, putting my pepperoni slice down in front of me.

"She's no one," I answered. "There is no lucky girl."

"She's Nick McKelty's cousin," Frankie added.

"Oh, that must be Joe McKelty's niece," said a man with a red beard sitting next to Papa Pete. "I went to my high-school prom with her mother."

Great. Now the whole city of New York was participating in my love life. I mean my *not* love life.

"Joe mentioned the girl to me," Harvey chimed in. "Tells me she plays the drums. Sounds like a spunky girl you've picked for yourself, Hank."

Attention! Is there anyone else in Harvey's who would like to comment on my relationship with Zoe McKelty?

Apparently there was. A woman wearing a knitted cap with two big pom-poms hanging down by her ears spoke up.

"Valentine's Day is coming up, honey," she said to me. "Buy her some flowers."

"Yeah," said the waiter, who had a tattoo of a peacock on his arm. "Chicks love roses."

"Forget roses," said the lady with the pom-poms. "Go orchids."

"I've had better luck with roses," the tattoo guy said. "Stick with roses, little dude."

This had got totally out of control. The whole restaurant was buzzing about something that hadn't even happened. I had to take some action.

"Thanks for all your advice and good wishes," I said in a voice loud enough so everyone could hear me, which, by the way, wasn't that loud because Harvey's only holds about twenty people. "But I'm not in love. I just met this girl-type person and she just happens to be a very nice girl-type person and that's all there is to it."

Good. That put an end to that.

Harvey brought over a lemonade and put it down in front of me. "Here you go, Romeo," he said, giving me a wink.

What was going on here? Harvey had never

winked at me before. Thank goodness Papa Pete came to my rescue. He could tell that I was definitely not comfortable with all the love talk.

"So, kids, let's change the subject," he said. "Tell me what happened in school today."

"School was regular," I began quickly, "except we have Mr Rock for a substitute for one whole month."

"Where's Ms Adolf?" Papa Pete asked. "Not sick, I hope."

"She threw her back out doing the rumba," Ashley said.

"Funny, she doesn't seem like the rumba type," Papa Pete said.

"Yeah," I agreed. "She seems more like the give-everyone-a-*D* type."

"Well, you can't judge a book by its cover," Papa Pete said. "Inside, Ms Adolf is obviously quite passionate and romantic."

Frankie, Ashley, and I almost spat out our pizza in unison.

"That is so gross, Papa Pete," I said. "That is the grossest thing you have ever said."

"Immediate change of subject," Frankie said. "Let's move right on to telling you about after school. No chance of Ms Adolf getting all passionate cropping up there."

"Fine," said Papa Pete, polishing off his doughnut. "What happened after school?"

"We're taking Tae Kwon Do," Ashley added. "Today was mostly a lecture on its history and stuff, but next week we're going to learn some basic moves and in a couple of weeks, Mr Love said we are going to participate in some exhibition matches."

"We are?" I said. Wow, maybe I left Tae Kwon Do too early. That was sounding like fun.

"You're coming back, aren't you, Zip?" Frankie said.

"Me? Coming back? Um ... yeah. Sure I am."

That's weird, Hank. Didn't you just tell Zoe that you were coming back to the Reading Gym?

"Good," Frankie said, "because I want you to be my sparring partner. We'll show them how it's done."

As I ate my slice of pizza, I wondered if it was possible to clone yourself and be in two places at once. I was going to have to look that up on the Internet the minute I got home.

CHAPTER 11

WHEN I GOT HOME, I raced into our apartment and dashed for my dad's laptop without even taking my jacket off. I didn't think that you could successfully clone yourself, but you never know what those scientists are coming up with. I figured it was worth a quick check on the computer. Unfortunately, my dad had already parked himself at the laptop that we keep on the dining room table, and he was hogging the screen as usual.

"Excuse me, Dad, but would it be OK if I look something up?" I asked as politely as I could.

"Sure, Hank, right after I fill in this eight-letter word for knee scab."

My dad has always been a crossword puzzle maniac, but lately he's become obsessed with online crossword puzzles. He competes non-stop with other crossword puzzle maniacs around the world, like in Africa and the South Pole and stuff.

"How was karate?" he asked, without looking up from the screen.

"It's Tae Kwon Do," I answered. "And it was fine."

"You learn any fancy moves?"

"Not yet. Mr Love is the sensei, and he's still giving us the history of martial arts. Next week we start the real stuff."

You've probably noticed that I didn't mention to my dad that I was thinking of doing the Reading Gym instead of Tae Kwon Do. It's not that I was trying to lie to him. Not exactly, anyway. I just figure there are some things he doesn't need to know. Like anything that has to do with my performance in school. If I had told him that I was taking the Reading Gym because Mr Rock recommended that I get special help, he would've got all upset and wanted to go and talk to Mr Rock about what's wrong with me. And then he'd start checking my progress every five minutes and supervising my extra work and telling me a million times a night how he thinks I should be working harder. I know because I've been through this with him before. I also know that the fastest way to get him to change any subject is to talk about crossword puzzles.

Which I immediately did.

"Does 'scrape' work?" I asked, looking over his shoulder at the screen as if all those little boxes and letters and numbers made any sense to me at all.

"Think about it, Hank. Scrape is only six letters."

Hey, I thought it was great that I came up with a word at all. When you spell like I do, you can't be too picky about the number of letters involved.

"Um ... what about 'icky skin'?" I suggested.

"That's two words, Hank. Not one."

"Besides," an annoying voice said from behind me, "skin is technically not a scab. Everyone knows a scab is composed of dried blood and the remains of dead skin cells."

This cheerful piece of news could only have been delivered by one person in my family, my know-it-all sister, Emily.

"Actually, while we're talking scabs, we can't leave out the black scab, which is a potato disease that causes mildew-type growth to spring up on the skin of the common potato."

I didn't even have to look around to see who was talking now. There is only one person on the planet both boring and disgusting enough to be fascinated with potato-skin scabs, and that would be my sister's bony little boyfriend, Robert Upchurch.

"Robert, you are so interesting," Emily said to him. "Imagine, I didn't know a thing about black scabs."

"Let's go and look them up in the encyclopaedia," Robert said. "Maybe there'll be an illustration of one we can trace and colour in."

I am not kidding you. This conversation actually took place in my own flat and was heard by my very own ears. Sometimes I wonder how Emily and I are related. One of us is a mutant throwback, I'm just not sure which one.

As Emily and Robert got up from their Scrabble game and hopped off into nerd land to read all about potato disease, Emily suddenly stopped and turned to me.

"Oh, I forgot," she said. "There was a phone call for you. A girl."

I tried not to look too interested, but I noticed that my heart sped up a little.

"Did she leave a name?" I asked, twirling the belt on my gi with what I hoped looked like a who-cares kind of attitude.

71

"Yes," Emily said.

Then she waited. That puny pigtailed punk was going to make me ask. Can you believe it?

"Would you care to share that piece of information with me, Emily?"

"Let's see," she said, with a wicked little grin. "I'm not sure I remember."

That did it. I lunged for her, but she's quick and dodged out of the way before I could reach her.

"Save me, Robert," she laughed. "Hank's attacking me!"

Yeah, like Robert could ever save her. The guy is as skinny as a flagpole and the only muscle he has in his whole body is in his tongue. And he got that one from talking so much about such attractive topics as black scabs and dust mites.

"Stop teasing your brother, Emily," my dad said. "The proper way to deliver a message includes date of call, time of call, name of caller and any and all message to be communicated."

"OK," Emily said, stifling a giggle. "February ninth, four forty-four p.m. Zoe McKelty called. She said to tell you she loves you."

My dad stopped typing. The living room grew very quiet.

I couldn't see my ears, but I'm pretty sure they turned bright red, along with everything else on my face.

"She didn't say that!" I said. "Did she?"

Emily burst out laughing, and Robert did too. When Robert laughs, it sounds like a hippo snorting up river water.

Now that my dad knew it was a joke, he started typing again.

"Emily!" he said, not looking up from his screen. (He must have had a brainwave on the knee scab front.) "Deliver the proper message."

"OK, OK," she answered. "Zoe McKelty called and said to tell you that you forgot your notebook. And your pen. And your root-beer-flavoured gummy worms."

That is so typical of me. Why can't I remember anything? Here I am trying to impress this girl with how cool I am, and what do I do? Leave my gummy worms behind.

Hank Zipzer, how uncool can you be?

"Is this young lady in your karate class?" my dad asked.

"Tae Kwon Do, Dad. And yes, she is."

My voice cracked a little on that last part because if I told him she was in Reading Gym then I'd have to bring up the whole subject and that wasn't going to happen. Again, I knew I had to change the subject as quickly as possible.

"Did she leave her number?" I asked Emily.

"Maybe," Emily answered. Then she whispered so my dad couldn't hear. "What's it worth to you?"

"My dessert every night for a week," I whispered back.

"Wow," said Emily. "Someone's really in love."

What was it with this love thing? I mean, a guy can make a friend, can't he?

I took Zoe's number, which Emily had written down on a Post-it note, grabbed the phone and headed into my room. Without thinking, I dialled the number. I should've thought about what I was going to say before I dialled, but I didn't, so when Zoe answered, I just kind of sat there on my bed, holding the phone.

"Hello," she said. "Is anyone there?"

"It's me," I finally stammered.

"Hi, me," she said with a laugh. "Me who?"

"Me, Hank Zipzer."

"Oh ... you mean Hank *Improvement* Zipzer."

"Huh?"

"You said Improvement was your middle name. Remember?"

I laughed. The problem was, after I started laughing, I couldn't stop. That happens sometimes when I get nervous. I either laugh too much or talk too much or eat too much or bite my nails too much.

Finally, I bit my lip really hard until it hurt, to make myself stop laughing.

"You forgot all your stuff in Reading Gym," Zoe said.

"Oh," was all I could think to say.

"Mr Rock was already gone, so I took it with me."

"Oh," I said again. My mouth couldn't seem to produce another sound.

"My uncle's picking me up from school tomorrow and taking me to his bowling alley," she went on. "I hang out there sometimes when my mum's at work."

"Oh."

That makes three oh's in a row. Come on, Hankster. Three strikes and you're out. You know that! Say something. Anything!

"So maybe you could meet me there tomorrow and pick up your stuff," Zoe said. "It's called

McKelty's Roll 'N' Bowl, and it's just around the corner from your school."

I go to McKelty's all the time with Papa Pete, who is a champion bowler and the leader of his league team, the Chopped Livers. The bowling alley is owned by Nick McKelty's dad, who is actually a very nice man in spite of the fact that he is the father of the world's biggest blowbag.

"Hank?" she said. "Hello? Are you there?"

Oops, I had forgotten to answer. I was so busy thinking about the Chopped Livers and Nick McKelty's dad and my three oh's in a row that my brain had gone into orbit and left my mouth here on planet Earth with nothing to say.

Yo, brain! Hank here. Over here on the bed. Yeah, that's me, the doofus holding this phone. If it's not too much trouble, can you come back to Earth sometime? Like NOW!!!!

"Hank?" Zoe said.

"Yeah, I'm here," I answered when the old brainster finally kicked into gear. "And I'll be there."

"Where?"

"McKelty's. Tomorrow. After school."

"Great. See you then. Bye, Hank."

The phone clicked. I just sat there on my bed,

holding the phone and listening to the dial tone. What a great girl that Zoe was.

Man, oh, man, she even had a great dial tone.

CHAPTER 12

I NEVER THINK ABOUT what I'm going to wear to school. As long as I have something covering the bottom of me, something covering the top of me and a couple of things covering my feet, I figure I'm good to go.

But I have to confess, the next morning was different. After I got up and brushed my teeth and combed my hair (sort of), I actually stood in front of my wardrobe and thought about what I was going to wear. I mean, I didn't put on a collared shirt or those black slithery dress-up socks I have to wear to family dinners in restaurants or anything. But I did pick out a new Mets sweatshirt and two socks that actually matched. After all, I didn't want Zoe to think I was so flaky that I couldn't match my socks *or* remember to take my gummy worms. I mean, a little flaky is cute. A lot flaky is ... well ... just too flaky.

"If it's OK with you, I'm not going to be home today until four o'clock," I told my mum at breakfast.

"Do you have another activity at school, honey?" she asked, dishing me up a big helping of her scrambled tofu with a stringy green thing in it. She's told me a million times what the stringy green thing is, but I keep forgetting the name. I only know two things about it. One, it's some kind of green thing, and two, it tastes way too green. Did I mention it was green?

Oh, come to think of it, that's what it is. Dandelion greens.

"I'm going to McKelty's Roll 'N' Bowl to meet a friend," I said, trying to sound super-duper casual.

I glanced over at Emily, who was sitting at the breakfast table with her pet iguana, Katherine, draped around her shoulder like a scaly green sweater.

"I'll bet he's meeting a *girl* friend," Emily said.

"Well, I think it's very lovely to have friends that are girls," my mum said, cool mum that she is.

Katherine's tongue shot out and snatched up a chunk of tofu from my plate.

"Your lizard's hungry," I said, trying to get Emily off the subject of my social life. "You should feed her more."

"Robert and I are baking Katherine some special iguana treats after school today," Emily said. "Parsnip and squash squares."

"That sounds delicious and nutritious," my mum said.

"Don't give Mum any ideas," I whispered to Emily. "These dandelion greens are bad enough. And if you want my dessert tonight, lay off the girlfriend talk when Dad comes in."

"That will cost you a chocolate mousse and three oatmeal biscuits," Emily said.

She drives a hard bargain, that Emily, but what choice did I have? My dad isn't the kind of guy you want to talk to about a crush, unless it involves a seven-letter synonym for one. So if Zoe was going to be my secret, and that meant paying Emily in chocolate mousse and oatmeal cookies to keep her mouth shut, then I guess that was how it had to be.

Frankie and Ashley and I always hang out together after school, so I needed to tell them that I was meeting Zoe at McKelty's instead of hanging with them. I was planning to break the news to them on the walk to school, but Emily and Robert tagged along that morning, and I wasn't in the mood to discuss it around them. The whole Zoe thing was way too much the topic of conversation for me.

Anyway, I decided to wait until lunchtime, when Frankie and Ashley and I could sit down and talk without fourth-grade ears listening in.

Frankie brought it up first.

"Hey, Zip," he said as we stood in the cafeteria lunch queue. "Ashweena and I decided we should all meet in the clubhouse at three-thirty to practise some Tae Kwon Do moves. Get a jump on old Mr Love."

"I can't today," I said, grabbing the two-taco special from under the glass and putting the plate on my tray without looking up. Boy, girl stuff does weird things to your head. Suddenly, I was uncomfortable talking with Frankie about my arrangement with Zoe. Frankie, who's been my best friend since we were born!

"You have an orthodontist appointment?" Ashley asked.

"Do you see any chocolate milk?" I answered.

"Booster shot?" Frankie asked.

"That's OK. I'll just get regular milk."

"Hank," Ashley said, pushing her glasses up on her nose so she could get a good look at me. "I notice you're not answering."

As we carried our trays to the table, she followed me, shooting out questions faster than I could answer them.

"Are you going shoe shopping? Are your library books due? Wait, are you getting a haircut? Seeing an educational therapist? Taking a Ping-Pong lesson? What?"

I sat down at the table and concentrated very hard on unfolding my napkin.

"Zip," Frankie said. "It's no big deal. Just tell us what you're doing after school."

"OK," I said, "but I don't want to have a major discussion about it. I'm meeting Zoe McKelty at the bowling alley."

"Well, check you out," Frankie said with a grin. "Hank Zipzer, ladies' man."

"Frankie, that's so immature," Ashley said. "I bet I know why they're meeting. Hank is going to tell Zoe that he's not coming back to the Reading Gym because he's taking Tae Kwon Do instead, and he doesn't want her to feel bad that she's stuck there doing boring stuff while we're having fun. Isn't that right, Hank?"

Yikes. I realized that I had never even mentioned to Frankie and Ashley that I was thinking of dropping out of Tae Kwon Do and taking Reading Gym instead. And I had told Zoe that I was staying in Reading Gym for sure. The cloning thing wasn't going to work out – which meant that unless I could come up with a new way to be in two places at once, I was in a pickle.

What I needed to do was just talk to Frankie and Ashley about my decision.

OK, Hankster. Just say the words. Tell them that you can't decide. That you may drop out of Tae Kwon Do. If you do, they'll understand. They're your friends.

I opened my mouth to discuss the situation with them, but instead, here's what came out.

"You're right, Ash. That's exactly what I'm going to tell Zoe. How'd you know that?"

"I knew it," said Ashley, "because you're such a sensitive guy, Hank. And that's just the kind of thing you'd do."

"Sensitive and starving," I said.

With that, I shoved a whole taco into my mouth. I figured that was one way to end the conversation.

What was going on with me? Was I truly

going to disappoint my friends and drop out of Tae Kwon Do, something I'd wanted to do since I was little? Of course I wasn't. That would be crazy. Was I truly going to leave Reading Gym, after I'd told Zoe I was staying? Of course I wasn't. That would be crazy.

I picked up the second taco and shoved it into my mouth in one bite.

"Wow, somebody's hungry," Ashley said.

"Hey, us martial arts guys need nourishment," Frankie said. "Isn't that right, Zip?"

I just nodded.

Suddenly, a big beefy hand came swooping down onto my tray and grabbed the chocolate chip cookie I had picked for dessert.

"Hey, that's mine!" I said, turning around just in time to see Nick McKelty shove my cookie into his mouth.

"Not any more," he answered, cookie crumbs spewing from his blubbery lips. At least, I think that's what he said. It's hard to understand a guy who's grinding up a jumbo-sized cookie all in one bite.

"You better get me another one, McKelty," I said.

"Hey, we can share now, Zipperhead. I mean,

we're almost like cousins."

"What are you talking about? I'm not related to you. No way."

"I hear you and my cousin Zoe are getting really ... um ... close."

"We're friends, McKelty. Ever heard the word?"

"Zoe said she thinks you're nice. Obviously, the girl has no taste."

I considered taking McKelty on, but then I decided that the best thing was to ignore him. The less I talked to him about Zoe, the better. I didn't want him telling her that I'm an idiot before she got a chance to know me. I mean, if she's going to think I'm an idiot, at least I want to earn that on my own.

McKelty had already lost interest in me, anyway. He had sniffed out a peanut butter cup sitting on Kim Paulson's tray and was stomping over to snag it. The guy is a food-grinding machine.

Strange as it seems, even that unpleasant encounter with McKelty couldn't bring down my spirits. I was in a great mood the whole afternoon. I didn't think about the Great Tae Kwon Do Versus the Reading Gym dilemma. I didn't think about report cards, which were coming out in two weeks. All I could think about was hanging out with Zoe after school. It was like the feeling you get when you know it's going to rain on Saturday and your favourite cartoon marathon is on all day. You can't wait because you know you're going to be eating cheese and crackers in front of the TV all day and everything is going to be perfect.

When the final bell rang, I grabbed my rucksack, ran down the stairs and raced out of the front door of the school. I passed Mr Love, who was standing on the steps, wearing a snowman scarf that featured two baby snowmen with fuzzy earmuffs balancing on a seesaw.

"Nice scarf, Mr Love," I said, waving goodbye to him.

And the funny thing was, I actually meant it. Those little baby snowmen were totally cute. OK, I know what you're thinking. Hank Zipzer has totally lost it. That Zoe McKelty has taken over his brain and turned him into a snowman-scarf-loving ding-dong. And you know what? I might actually have to agree with you on that point.

I was heading to McKelty's Roll 'N' Bowl, which is not even two blocks away from my school, when suddenly I got a brilliant idea. I turned around and took a detour over to Broadway. Three doors past Harvey's is Babka's, my favourite bakery in all of New York. I walked in and found Trudi, my favourite bakery salesperson in all of New York, standing behind the counter.

"I know what you want," Trudi said to me. "A black-and-white cookie, right?"

Trudi knows that the black-and-white cookie is what I consider to be the Grand Poobah of all desserts.

"Actually, Trudi, today I want *two* black-and-white cookies," I said with a smile.

"That's a mysterious grin," she said. "Something tells me the other cookie must be for someone very special. You got a girl, Hank?"

Hey, was I wearing a sign on my back that said, "Please talk to me about very personal things?" I must have been, because everyone sure felt comfortable doing it.

I took the little white paper bag with my two cookies and placed it carefully in the upper pouch of my rucksack. A black-and-white is a delicate thing, and I didn't want to give Zoe a crumbled-up one. As I walked the two blocks over to McKelty's, I visualized what was about to happen next. I'd give Zoe her cookie and we'd sit down in a booth. As we munched, we'd listen to the sound of the bowling balls rolling down the alleys and the clatter of the pins falling down. Hopefully, I'd be able to think of something more to say than "oh" – something that would make her laugh and flash those turquoise braces of hers.

I was feeling totally great when I climbed up the stairs to McKelty's Roll 'N' Bowl and pushed open the heavy red leather door. My eyes scanned the room for Zoe. She wasn't in the video game area. She wasn't in the coffee shop. She wasn't behind the desk, where her uncle Joe was handing out a pair of shoes to one of the customers.

Wait, there she was. In one of the beaten-up leather booths by the alleys, just like I imagined she'd be. Sitting there, smiling, wearing her funny little hat, waiting for me to arrive.

Only one thing was different than I had imagined it to be.

Sitting right next to her in the booth, chowing down a greasy cheeseburger and letting the ketchup squirt out of his big, sloppy mouth, was the idiot himself, none other than Nick the Tick McKelty.

Hey, who invited him?

CHAPTER 13

TEN THINGS I WAS CONSIDERING
SAYING TO NICK MCKELTY TO GET
HIM OUT OF THAT BOOTH

1. Why don't you make like a tree and leaf?
2. What are you doing here? Did someone leave your cage open?
3. I'd like to invite you somewhere special. It's called outside.
4. I hate to see you go, but I'd love to watch you leave.
5. I thought they only allowed humans in here.
6. Why don't you go to the library and brush up on your ignorance?
7. Before I saw you I was hungry. Now I'm fed up.
8. I'm very busy now. Can I ignore you some other time?

9. I'd like to help you out. Which way did you come in?
10. King Kong's calling you. He wants his face back.

Hank's note: Feel free to vote and select what you would say to Nick if you were me. You can check your answer on the next page.

CHAPTER 14

"HEY, MCKELTY," I SAID. "What are you doing here? Did someone leave your cage open?"

"Very funny, Zipperbutt," he said. "So funny I'm not even cracking a smile."

"I'd like to help you out, Nick. Which way did you come in?"

Zoe laughed. There they were, those turquoise braces.

"What are you, some kind of comedian?" McKelty said, spraying a combo of ketchup and mustard and pickle juice from the space between his front teeth.

"You know, before I saw you I was hungry," I said. "Now I'm just fed up."

Zoe started to laugh really hard now, which made McKelty even more irritated.

"Me and my cheeseburger are out of here," he said. "I don't need to hang around with a loser like you."

"Excellent idea, Nick. Why don't you make like a tree and leaf?"

The big lug scooped up his messy cheeseburger remains, slid out of the booth and stomped off. As he left, I called after him, "Why don't you go to the library and brush up on your ignorance?"

(In case you were keeping track, I used numbers two, nine, seven, one and six from the list ... in that order. Hey, there was no rule that I could use only one, was there?)

Zoe was laughing so hard she had tears in her eyes. "My cousin Nick can dish it out, but he sure can't take it," she said.

"What's it like being related to someone like that?" I asked her. "Does he ever get nice?"

"I don't know him all that well," Zoe said. "We just moved back to New York from Seattle because my mum got a new job here. We left when I was a baby, so I've only known Nick for a month or so."

"I've known him my whole life," I said.

"So he told me."

"I bet he told you I was a jerk and a loser," I said, sliding into the booth next to her.

"And an idiot and a moron and a knuckle-head," she said.

"Wow, he was really on a roll."

I didn't know what to say then. I mean, how do you tell someone that you're not a moron, especially when a lot of times you actually think you are a moron? I could tell her that I've always had trouble in school, and ever since Nick figured that out way back in kindergarten, he's been calling me names. I could tell her that I think kids who call other kids names because they have trouble in school are nothing but bullies. I could tell her that...

Earth to Hank. Get your brain back on track, buddy. Remember, you were having a conversation. It's been a while since you've said anything.

I looked over at Zoe, embarrassed that my thoughts had carried me off to Jupiter while she was still there on planet Earth. But she didn't seem to notice that I had been missing in action. She was listening to the music playing over the speakers and drumming out the beat on the table.

"I want to be a drummer when I grow up," she said.

"You're already a drummer," I said. "You play the table better than anyone I know."

"You're funny, Hank. It's going to be so cool

93

to be in Reading Gym together. We'll have a great time, won't we?"

Uh-oh. This was the moment. Decision time.

I closed my eyes and imagined two pictures of myself. In one, I was wearing my gi and delivering a powerful roundhouse kick. I looked awesome. In the other, I was sitting at a library desk, reading a book. I looked ... well ... way less awesome. Which one was the real Hank?

Face it, Hank. You're a martial arts guy.

There it was. Decision made.

OK, so this was the time to tell Zoe that I was going back to Tae Kwon Do class. That I was changing my middle name from "Improvement" to "The Smasher."

"Yeah ... about Reading Gym, Zoe. I was thinking that..."

Before I could finish the sentence, who should come galumphing up to our booth but Nick the Tick. He was holding a bowling ball in his ketchupy hand.

"I challenge you, Zipperbutt," he said. "One ball each. Whoever knocks the most pins down gets to stay. The loser guy has to leave. Pick your ball and meet me on lane seven, Loser Guy."

He stomped off before I could say no.

"This will be fun," Zoe said, jumping up from the booth. "I bet you can beat him, Hank."

"No problemo," I said out loud, but inside I was saying, "Yes, problemo."

I am not too good on the athletic front. Frankie is a great athlete – he's good at anything that involves a ball. Me, I'm a good swimmer. And a pretty good Ping-Pong player. And if you promise never to tell a soul, I'll also share with you that I can do some complicated ballroom dancing steps that my mum taught me. But when it comes to baseballs and footballs and basketballs and other round objects, including bowling balls, I'm not the most talented guy on the team. McKelty knows that too, which I'm sure is why he challenged me to a bowling duel.

Before I could explain any of that to Zoe, she was heading over to lane seven. I had no choice but to accept Nick's challenge.

I grabbed the first ball I saw on the rack and instantly fell smack on the ground. There must have been rocks inside that thing! It felt like it weighed two tons. After checking my arm to make sure it hadn't stretched to twice its length, I grabbed another ball, a lighter one this time. In case you're wondering how I knew it was lighter, it was because it was orange with yellowish swirly designs all over it.

I know, I know. This wasn't the manliest ball on the rack. But I could pick it up and throw it without hurling myself down the alley, and I figured in a bowling duel, that had to be more important than the colour scheme.

When I reached lane seven, McKelty was there tying his bowling shoes and Zoe was sitting at the score table.

"I can't do this. I don't have the right shoes," I said.

"You can just bowl in your socks," McKelty said.

"That's against the rules," I pointed out.

"It's one ball, dingbat. Besides, my dad makes the rules and if anyone questions him, he'll go directly to his best friend who happens to be the first cousin of the mayor of Brooklyn. So there."

I wasn't in the mood to hear him rattle on about the McKelty Factor, which is truth times ten, so I just took off my shoes without answering. I accidentally on purpose waved my feet around in front of Zoe, just to make sure she noticed that I was wearing matching socks. A guy has to play to his strengths, you know.

McKelty decided to go first, which was fine with me. He held the bowling ball up in front of his face and stared at the ten pins at the far end of the alley, making a big deal out of how seriously he was aiming. Then he took a few steps, swung his arm back, brought it forward and let the ball fly.

I have to admit, it was a pretty powerful performance. That ball went careening down the lane, straight and fast and dead-on centre. When it hit the pins, they clattered loudly and nine of them fell down. The last pin standing wobbled back and forth, tipping to one side then the other.

"Fall over, stupid!" McKelty shouted to the pin.

It was like the pin heard his voice and said to itself, "You can't talk to me like that," because it stopped wobbling and stood straight and tall in its corner of the lane.

"Nine," said Zoe. "Pretty good, Nick, but beatable. Isn't that right, Hank?"

"No problemo," I said. And I think by now we all know that when I say that it means, "Yes, problemo."

I picked up my orange and yellow swirly ball and walked to the starting position. They must have put oil or wax on the floor, because I noticed how slippery the wood was under my socks. I made a mental note to be careful not to slide.

I held the ball up to my face, just as Nick had done and stared down the lane at the ten pins. Then I took a few steps forward and got up a little speed. Actually, I got up a lot of speed. Way too much speed. I couldn't stop myself, and those few steps turned into an all-out slide. I went sailing down the lane like an Olympic speed skater, clutching onto my orange swirly ball with one hand and waving my other arm wildly in the air to try to keep my balance.

It wasn't pretty, folks.

"Attention, bowler on lane seven!" Joe's voice came over the speaker so loudly you could probably hear him on the top of the Statue of Liberty. "There is no walking, sliding or whatever the heck you're doing allowed on the lanes."

What did he think? I was trying to look like a total idiot on purpose?

Thankfully, I finally came to a stop before I reached the pins. It would have been really terrible if I had knocked down the pins and kept sliding all the way through to the other side. Now that I mention it, what exactly is on the other side of the pins, anyway? I'll have to check that out someday.

I was stuck in an awkward situation. If I wasn't allowed to walk on the lane, how was I supposed to get back?

I had no choice but to take the gutter route.

Let me tell you, it's not easy to hustle your rear end down the gutter of a bowling alley. It's slippery and curvy and the whole time you're worrying that you're going to get clipped by a returning bowling ball coming down the gutter.

When I finally got back to the score table, I thought for sure Zoe would be laughing her head off at me. Nick the Tick certainly was.

"Zipperhead, that was pathetic," he howled.

Zoe wasn't laughing, though. "I think you need to put your shoes on," she said. "It's dangerous out there in just your socks."

Wow. Not only didn't she laugh at me, she actually had a helpful suggestion. That was really sweet.

I put my regular shoes back on, picked up the orange ball and took my position at the head of the lane.

Concentrate, Hank. You have to score a ten to beat McKelty. You can do this if you look, think and most of all, concentrate.

I took aim, swung my arm back, brought it forward and let the ball loose.

"Go," I whispered to myself. "Go! Go! Go!"

CHAPTER 15

DON'T GET YOUR HOPES UP, GUYS. This is a Hank Zipzer book, not a superhero comic where Captain Bowler pulls out an incredible move just in the nick of time. Remember, it's me. Just plain Hank.

The ball took its good old time to reach the pins. By the time it got there, it was teetering on the edge of the lane, right next to the gutter.

Fortunately, it didn't roll into the gutter until it had knocked down one pin, the one on the very, very outside. I watched that pin wobble for what seemed like forever, hoping that as it fell it would take down the other nine pins.

No such luck.

I scored a one.

"Bye-bye, Zipper Klutz," McKelty said, handing me my rucksack.

I was too embarrassed to even look at Zoe. I just grabbed my stuff and ran out of the door without even saying goodbye.

CHAPTER 16

THE PHONE WAS RINGING when I burst into my apartment. The minute I heard it, I hoped it was Zoe, telling me not to be embarrassed because she isn't a very good bowler either. Telling me to come back and get my notebook which I had forgotten to pick up. Telling me that Nick was a jerk and I was just the kind of guy she truly admired.

"It's for you," Emily said, handing me the phone. "And it's a girl."

Yes! It *was* Zoe! No other girl ever calls me.

"Hi, Zoe," I said.

"Uh ... Hank?" said the voice on the other end of the phone. "Sorry to disappoint you, but it's me, Mr Rock."

I looked over at Emily, and she was holding her sides, laughing. Wait until I was off the phone. I was going to get her good. I was going to tell Dad on her the minute he came out of ...

out of wherever he was.

"Mr Rock," I said into the phone. "I'm sorry. My sister said you were a girl."

"Well, your sister needs to take a science lesson." Mr Rock laughed.

Emily was still laughing when she walked back to the dining-room table where Robert was holding Katherine and trying to feed her one of the parsnip and squash squares they had baked. I figured those stinky squares were probably why our entire apartment smelled like the inside of a rotten-vegetable bin. Katherine hissed at Robert every time he tried to shove an iguana treat near her snout.

"Do you want to talk to me or to my dad?" I asked Mr Rock. Most of the time, if a teacher calls our house, they're calling to tell my parents that I messed up on something. So I just figured he was calling for my dad.

"Actually, it's you I'd like to speak with," Mr Rock said. "I was wondering if you had made a decision on whether to continue with Reading Gym."

"Reading Gym seems like fun, Mr Rock. Really and truly it does. But I promised Frankie and Ashley that I'd stick with Tae Kwon Do."

"Are you sure about this decision, Hank?"

"See, I promised Frankie I'd be his sparring partner. He's counting on me."

"As I said to you in school, Hank, although I highly recommend the Reading Gym, in the end it's your choice. If you're sure of your decision, I'll go ahead and assign a new partner to Zoe. See you tomorrow, Hank."

"Wait! Mr Rock! Did you say I was going to be Zoe's partner?"

"Yes. She requested you."

"As in 'I'd like to work with Hank.'"

"Exactly."

"She really said that?"

"Yes."

"Mr Rock, could you hold on a minute, please?"

I covered up the phone and started to pace. Emily and Robert both stopped their parsnip-squash feeding frenzy and stared at me. Even Katherine took a break from her hissing and focused her bulgy, beady eyes on me. Our dog, Cheerio, ran back and forth with me, staying right in between my legs, so that I nearly tripped over him with every step I took. Everyone, human, reptile and cute little four-legged furry guy, was feeling my dilemma.

"Tae Kwon Do versus Reading Gym," I whispered out loud, pacing back and forth.

"If you ask me, reading is pretty important," Emily said.

Then she did a weird thing. She came over to me and put her hand on my shoulder, in a nice, friendly kind of way. "Plus, you seem to really like Zoe. And it seems like she did request you."

Was this Emily the Annoying being Emily the Helpful?

Robert came over to me and put his scrawny little hand on my other shoulder. Man, this was getting too weird.

"Love is what makes the world go round, Hank," he said, looking all gaga-eyed at Emily. Then he got hold of himself and turned back into Super Nerd. "Love and orbital force, of course."

Cheerio looked up at me and yipped. I don't speak dog, but I think I saw him smiling with his bottom teeth. Could he be nodding yes?

I put the phone up to my ear.

"OK, Mr Rock. I'm in."

"In what, Hank? I need you to commit."

"Get out the trampoline and fire up the pommel horse, I'm going to Reading Gym."

"That's a good decision, Hank. You're a smart kid. See you tomorrow."

He hung up, and suddenly, there I was, with Emily's hand on one shoulder and Robert's on the other. That was unacceptable.

"OK, guys, the love fest is over," I said. "Besides, Katherine is hissing for you."

The junior science brigade went back to their parsnip party and Cheerio rolled over for a belly scratch. I think he was proud of me too. Either that or his belly just itched.

"By the way, Emily, don't discuss this with Dad," I said as I scratched Cheerio.

"Why not? I'm sure he'd rather you learn to read than learn to fight."

"I have my reasons," I said.

"OK," Emily said. "But this will cost you. You make my bed all week."

"That's ridiculous. No deal."

"Dad!" Emily called out. "Hank has something to tell you."

A second later, my dad stuck his head out of the kitchen. "What is it, Hank?" he asked.

Emily looked over at me and smiled.

"OK, deal," I said.

"Hank just wanted to tell you that we both

106

think Katherine really likes you," she said.

"That's good," my dad said. "Tell Katherine I like her too. Now can I go back to my crossword?"

"Sure," said Emily. "Thanks, Dad."

Even though I had Emily's word to keep it a secret, I couldn't really feel comfortable with my decision until I told Frankie and Ashley that I was dropping out of martial arts. I decided to do it right away, like plunging into a freezing ocean all at once, rather than edging yourself in one inch at a time.

I took the lift to the basement, where we have our clubhouse in the storeroom next to the laundry. Frankie and Ashley had said they'd be down there practising some Tae Kwon Do.

I tiptoed by the laundry room, trying my best to avoid running into whatever adult was in there. I find that when adults are folding towels, they get very talkative and like to tell you about how far they walked to school when they were growing up and what their mum used to cook for their special birthday dinners. I don't know what it is about warm towels. They just bring out memories, I guess.

I thought I was safely past the laundry-room

door when our neighbour, Mrs Fink, stuck her head out into the hall. She was in her fluffy pink dressing gown and her fluffy pink matching slippers. That might sound like a weird thing to be wearing at four-thirty in the afternoon, but I understood it. It was a cold February day and personally, I think it's really fun on a cold day to bundle up in warm pyjamas and hang out in a toasty place, which the laundry room certainly was.

"Hank!" she said. "Come in and say hi while I finish folding the towels."

"Gee, Mrs Fink, I'd really like to, but Frankie and Ashley are waiting for me and it's kind of an emergency."

"Nothing wrong, I hope?"

"Oh no, it's not a *something's-wrong* kind of emergency, more of a *we-have-to-talk* kind of emergency."

"You go on your way, then, darling. And stop by my apartment later for a piece of my apple-cinnamon sugar cake. I remember my mother always made it for my special birthday dinners..."

What'd I tell you? It's the warm towels.

As I headed down the hall, I wondered if someday when I was folding towels and ran into a kid, I'd tell him about how my mum always made me tofu scramble with dandelion greens on special days. Somehow, it didn't jump out at you like apple-cinnamon sugar cake.

When I walked into the clubhouse, Frankie was sprawled on the big flowered couch, and Ashley was crumpled up in a ball on the floor. They were both wearing their gis.

"This looks more like Tae Kwon Don't than Tai Kwon Do," I said.

They both cracked up. At least, Frankie did and I was pretty sure Ashley did because I could see her ponytail shaking as it rested on her back.

Sure, you guys are laughing now, but wait until I flake out on you. Will you be laughing then?

"I'm beat," Frankie said. "Practising these moves is hard work. You wait and see."

Ashley spoke from her curled-up ball. "My arms are sore, my legs are sore, my feet are sore, even my forehead is sore."

"That's because Ashweena's no match for me," Frankie said. "I need you, Zip, to be a real partner."

OK, Hank. You're on. Open your mouth and let it fly.

"So about that partner thing," I said. "I think I'm deciding ... no ... I've for sure decided that I'm not going to do the Tae Kwon Do class. I'm taking Reading Gym instead."

Ashley uncurled herself from the ball and looked at Frankie. He looked at me and then back at her. It was very quiet in the clubhouse.

"I know you guys are disappointed," I said, talking really fast, "but it's just that I stink at reading and Mr Rock says that I need practice or..."

"Zip," Frankie said. "Stop."

"Not another word," Ashley agreed.

Wow, Hank, they must be really mad at you to not even let you explain.

"I think it's cool that you're getting reading help," Frankie said.

"And I think it's cool that you found Zoe to share the class with," Ashley said.

"So you guys aren't mad at me?" I said softly.

"Not even a little," Ashley answered.

Frankie gave me a thumbs-up sign. "You got to do what you got to do, Zip."

"One more thing," I added. "I'm not telling my dad about the switch. You know how upset he gets when he thinks I need special help. So as far as he knows, we're all doing Tae Kwon Do together."

"My lips are sealed," Frankie said, pretending to zip up his lips.

"Your secret is my secret," Ashley agreed.

Suddenly, I felt like the luckiest guy in the world. I mean, think of it. I had two best friends who understood me and really and truly wanted what was best for me. I had a hat-wearing drum-playing girl who had requested me as her reading partner. I had two matching socks and a new Mets sweatshirt. And I had knocked down a bowling pin without pulling my arm out of its socket.

I sat down with Frankie and Ashley and told them all about my meeting with Zoe. I told them all the things I said to McKelty, and they were so proud of my quick wit, although Frankie did give me a lecture about using an orange swirly ball in public. We laughed until our stomachs hurt.

After a while, Mrs Fink stuck her head in and gave us all big slices of her apple-cinnamon sugar cake.

Some days just work out perfectly.

CHAPTER 17

MY SPURT OF HAPPINESS kept right on going for the next month.

Ms Adolf's rumba injury was still keeping her home in bed, so she wasn't around to make us participate in her usual fun activities like pop quizzes and mini-tests and end-of-chapter questions and extra homework assignments.

It was great to have Mr Rock for a substitute teacher. He told at least one joke every day in class. And if you messed up on a test, he gave you a chance to study harder and take it again. Using his system, I got two *B*'s and a *C*-plus. Those grades actually got my dad to look up from his online crossword puzzle and say, "Much improved, Hank. Keep it up." And coming from him, that's a major compliment.

Tuesday quickly became my favourite day of the week. After school, Frankie and Ashley would change into their gis and go into the gym for Tae

Kwon Do. Zoe and I would meet in the library for Reading Gym. We were partners, helping each other put together our autobiographies.

I decided to make mine a scrapbook type of thing, because writing a really long essay was totally impossible for me. I brought in cool stuff from home, like photos and my drawing doodles and tickets from Mets games and the first poem I ever wrote. Mr Rock said it was OK to make a scrapbook, as long as I used everything that was there to practise my reading and spelling skills.

Being a drummer, Zoe decided to do a multimedia presentation. She wrote about her life in words that sounded like song lyrics. After each piece of writing, she made a tape of her favourite music from that time. She actually recorded herself singing "Wheels on the Bus" like a three-year-old and "Itsy Bitsy Spider" like a five-year-old. When she presented her autobiography to the class, she was going to keep time with the music using her drumsticks.

Now that's a creative person, wouldn't you agree?

The only problem in this otherwise very perfect month was that there were a few glitches in my plan not to tell my dad that I had switched out of Tae Kwon Do. Don't worry, he didn't find out, because Emily kept her mouth shut (although she did get an extra week of bed-making out of me). But I had a lot of close calls because when you're keeping something from your mum or dad, you can easily get caught. Trust me on that.

Like every Tuesday, I had to switch into my gi before I got home from school, so it looked like I had been in martial arts. Usually, I changed clothes in the gym bathroom, but one day I forgot. I walked home, rode up in the lift and was about to put the key into our apartment door when I realized I was still in my regular school clothes and my gi was in my rucksack.

I couldn't go back down to Frankie or Ashley's to change, because their parents were already home and they'd wonder why I was changing in their apartment. I couldn't go into the lift to change, because what if it stopped on another floor and when the door opened I was standing there with no clothes on? Try explaining that to Mrs Park on the fourth floor!

So I did the only thing a person could do. I decided to change right there in the hall. I was going to have to be quick, because one thing you don't want to do in the hall of your apartment building is stand around half naked. It's considered bad manners.

I took my gi out of my rucksack and laid it out in front of me on the floor. My plan was to take my jeans off first and replace them with the gi bottoms. Then I'd do the top part. That way, if the worst happened and someone saw me, at least I'd always be half covered.

I took a deep breath, so I could concentrate with all my might. Then, like a track star coming off the blocks, I pulled off my jeans and jumped into the gi bottoms. I did pull off one shoe in the process, but all in all, I was pretty pleased with how quickly my bottoms went on. Now all I had to do was get the top part changed, and I was home free.

I took another deep breath, yanked off my sweatshirt and my T-shirt and tossed them on the floor. Brrr, it was freezing cold. But before I could even reach for my gi top, the door across the hall opened and little Tyler King stepped out. He's five, and he was wearing his Spiderman pyjamas like he always does.

"Hi, Tyler," I said, trying to sound really casual, as though hanging around in the hall with no T-shirt on in the middle of a snowy February day was something I did all the time.

"Why are you naked, Hank?" he asked.

"I'm not naked, Tyler. I'm just not wearing a shirt."

"That's fun. I'm going to take my shirt off, too," he said, pulling off his Spiderman pyjama top.

"No, Tyler," I said. "It's cold. You have to put your shirt on."

"But you don't have one on."

"That's because I'm a big boy," I said.

OK, I know it was a lame answer, but I was under a lot of pressure.

I reached out and picked up his pyjama top. "Come on, let's put this on. Arms up."

"No!" he said.

"Look up there, Tyler," I said, pointing to the ceiling. "It's Spiderman!"

He looked up and I took the opportunity to slip his pyjama top over his head.

"I don't see Spidey, Hank!"

"That's because he's over there now," I said, pointing to the lift. "Can you wave to him?"

Tyler waved, and while his arm was out, I slid the pyjama arm over his arm. One down, one to go.

"Now he's over there, on the other side. Wave to Spiderman, Tyler. Say 'hi, Spidey'!"

Tyler waved, and I managed to get the pyjamas over his other arm. At least he was dressed, but now he was sad.

"I didn't see him, Hank! Did Spidey leave?"

"I think he went into your apartment, Tyler. Back inside the TV where he lives."

"I'm coming, Spiderman!" Tyler yelled. "Be right there."

He turned around, ran back inside his apartment and slammed the door.

Phew! That was hard. And cold. I took a second to recover, still with no top on, when I saw the other apartment door on our floor open just a crack.

"What's going on out here?" Mrs Fink said, peeking out from her door. "Hank, is that you? Where's your shirt? You'll freeze out there!"

"Sshhhhhhhh," I whispered to Mrs Fink. She's not known for speaking quietly, and the last thing I wanted was for my dad to hear her and come outside.

"What's with the 'sshhhhhhhh'? You have a secret?" she asked.

"Yes."

"Tell me," she said. "I love secrets."

I heard footsteps in my apartment, coming towards the door. I had two seconds, maximum, before they reached me. I had to come up with something. And quickly!

CHAPTER 18

*FIVE POSSIBLE SECRETS I COULD
TELL MRS FINK TO GET HER
TO CLOSE THE DOOR*

1. I am trying out for a Speed Clothes Changing contest, but I can't tell my family because I want to surprise them with my trophy.
2. I have a rare disease called Shirt Off Syndrome that causes me to pull my shirt off in weird places like hallways and supermarket aisles.
3. I suddenly got allergic to my shirt and if I didn't get it off right away, I would break out in hives as big as strawberries.
4. I decided to become a nudist, but I chickened out, so I'm becoming a half-nudist instead.
5. I am rehearsing for a school play in which

I have to play an ancient Siamese king, and everyone knows ancient Siamese kings didn't wear shirts.

CHAPTER 19

I HAD NO TIME to make a good decision, so I just blurted out the first thing that popped into my mind. "I'm in a Speed Clothes Changing contest," I told Mrs Fink. "Don't tell my family, because I want to surprise them with the trophy."

"Oh," Mrs Fink said. "How exciting. I'll make you a lemon poppy-seed cake when you win."

I pulled the top of my gi on and tied the belt just as my front door opened. It was my dad.

I tried to assume a really relaxed pose, like someone who had been sweating up a storm in his gi all afternoon.

"Hey, Dad."

"Hank, why didn't you just come in?" he asked. "And why do you only have one shoe on?"

Oops. I forgot about the shoe. Trust my dad to notice.

"I asked him to take it off," Mrs Fink said, "so I could see his sock. I think I found a matching one left in the dryer."

Nice recovery, Mrs Fink. Way to go.

"Oh," my dad said. "Well, come on in, Hank. You can show me what you learned in karate."

I glanced at Mrs Fink as I went inside, and she gave me a big wink.

"Let me know when I should get started on the lemon cake," she whispered.

Things didn't go that much smoother inside the apartment. My dad meant it when he asked to see what I'd been learning in karate. He sat down in his rocking chair and put his feet up on the coffee table.

"So show me some karate," he said.

"Well, first of all, Dad, it's Tae Kwon Do."

"Right," he said. "You've mentioned that. So, have you learned any kicks or blocks you can show me?"

"Oh, all kinds," I said. "But they're not really things you can do by yourself. You need a sparring partner for that kind of thing."

"Call up Frankie," my dad said. "Maybe he'll come up and you boys can show me what you're learning."

I went to the phone and dialled Frankie's number.

"Hey," I said when he answered the phone. "My dad wants us to show him what we're learning in Tae Kwon Do. Can you come up?"

"Are you crazy, Zip? You're not in Tae Kwon Do, therefore you haven't learned squat in Tae Kwon Do. What are we supposed to show him?"

I grinned at my dad, and gave him a thumbs-up sign.

"I know you have a lot of homework," I said into the phone, "so we'll just show him one or two moves and then you can get to work."

"Listen, Zip," Frankie said. "If you want to keep what you're doing from your dad, that's your business. But don't get me in the middle of it. That is not fair."

"Oh," I said, looking at my dad. "That's right. I forgot about the essay on the Constitution. Sure, I know you'll be up all night finishing it."

"You're really something, Zip," said Frankie. "Tell him whatever you want. I'll see you tomorrow."

I hung up the phone and flopped down on the sofa.

"No deal," I said to my dad. "Frankie says

he'd love to show you some stuff, but he has a lot of work to do on the history essay that's due tomorrow."

"What history essay?" my dad asked. "I didn't know you had one due tomorrow."

Uh-oh. Now I had really got myself into a corner. Of course, we didn't have an essay due – I made it up on the phone with Frankie. But now my dad thought we did have an essay due the next day. And there's nothing he likes better than to supervise me while I'm writing an essay.

If you think lying is easy, let me just tell you this. I had to spend the whole night in my room, writing an essay on the Constitution that was never even assigned.

I tell you, friends. Think twice before you tell your parents a story.

CHAPTER 20

EVERY THURSDAY, Zoe and I would meet at McKelty's Roll 'N' Bowl to have a root beer and do some extra work on our Reading Gym project. Most Thursdays, Frankie and Ashley came along too, and did their homework while we did ours.

One day, we were sitting at the usual booth in McKelty's when Nick came up to us.

"Hey, Zipper Dork, I challenge you to a bowling duel," he said. "Are you in the mood for losing?"

"I can't right now, Nick," I said. "I'm doing my schoolwork."

"Come on. The loser buys the winner a root beer."

"That doesn't work," I said. "There's four of us and only one root beer, so let's just forget it."

He wasn't letting me off the hook so easily.

"Tell you what," McKelty said. "If I lose, which is not going to happen, I'll buy all four of you root beers. If you lose, you buy me a root-beer float, some red licorice and a chunky chocolate bar."

I figured that was a typical snack for him. One thing you could definitely say about Nick McKelty was that he had a giant sweet tooth.

Frankie got up from the booth and stretched to his full tall-bodied self.

"My pal Hank is busy right now, Nick, but it just so happens that I've finished my homework, so I'll take you on," he said.

McKelty's face turned purple. It's one thing to challenge me, Hank Zipzer, to a competition, but it's a whole other deal to challenge Frankie Townsend. Frankie had been telling me how McKelty was always challenging everyone in their Tae Kwon Do class to a match – everyone but him, that is. McKelty's the kind of guy that likes to pick on people weaker than him, but will never stand up to someone he thinks is better.

"Come to think of it, my thumb is kind of sore," McKelty sputtered. "It's probably best if I give it a rest."

"Your thumb looks fine to me," Frankie said. "Come on, dude. I could use a little exercise."

Before McKelty had a chance to think of

another lame excuse, all of us had scooted over to the first available lane and taken a seat at the score table. This bowling duel was going to be fun to watch.

Let me just say two things about what followed.

One: There were no orange swirly balls at this match, thank goodness.

Two: I really enjoyed that root beer afterwards. It tasted especially sweet.

CHAPTER 21

THE FOLLOWING WEEK, Mr Love announced that the first exhibition matches would be taking place in Tae Kwon Do class.

Ashley was paired up with Joelle Atkins. Joelle loves her mobile phone so much that none of us thought she'd be able to stop talking on it long enough to take part in the match.

"That's fine with me," Ashley said. "I'll sneak up on her while she's speed-dialling."

Frankie was paired up with the blowbag himself, Nick McKelty. For the whole week before, McKelty had been telling everyone that he was going to take Frankie down. Even though McKelty weighed twice what Frankie did, I knew there was no way he could beat him. Frankie moves at the speed of light. McKelty moves at the speed of a snail. A really slow snail.

As I sat in Reading Gym that week, writing captions underneath the photos in my scrapbook and double-checking to make sure I used capital letters for all the proper nouns, I could hear the kids across the hall getting ready for the match. They were sliding chairs around the gym, and Mr Love was shouting out directions in his overly deep voice. A few times, Zoe and I got out of our seats and went to the door so we could hear what he was saying.

"Make a circle, young masters," he called out, "so we can gather in a circular shape, which, as we all know, is the best shape to gather in when sitting in a circle."

"I must have big-time learning challenges," Zoe said with a laugh, "because I don't understand anything your head teacher says."

"What's even more scary is that I *did* understand him," I said. "He's telling the kids to sit down so the matches can start."

We went back into the library to continue our work. Zoe was sitting at a computer, watching an animated purple dog trot in and out of his doghouse on the screen. It was an exercise to build up her tracking eye muscles.

"I wish we could go see the matches," Zoe said, looking up from the screen. "I'd love to see how Frankie and Ashley and Nick do. Besides, this yapping purple dog is getting on my nerves."

My hand shot up in the air.

"Do you need some help, Hank?" Mr Rock asked, walking quickly over to me. He had been working with Luke Whitman, whose nose was running like a tap. Judging from the fast pace he was setting to get to me, I think Mr Rock wanted a break from the mucus flow.

"It's about the Tae Kwon Do class, Mr Rock. They're having their first matches today. Please can we go?"

"What about your capital letters, Hank?"

"I'll finish them tonight at home. I promise."

"Hank, we have work to do in Reading Gym," Mr Rock said. "You guys are going to start the presentations of your life stories next week, and you need time to prepare."

"But Frankie and Ashley are competing today," I said. "I need to support my friends, don't I?"

"My cousin Nick is participating too," Zoe said, "and I know he'd like me there. I think being a close family is very important, don't you, Mr Rock?"

Way to go, Zoe McKelty. Play the old close family card!

Mr Rock scratched his chin and thought. "If I let you go, I have to offer the same opportunity to the rest of the group," he said.

"How about if those of us who go write a report about it?" I said. "For reading and writing practice."

"I guess I could live with that," Mr Rock said. "OK, kids, who else wants to go?"

Oddly enough, Zoe and I were the only two who raised our hands. The Wilson sisters, Kacey and Sloane, had a brother named Austin in Tae Kwon Do, but they said they saw plenty of him at home and watching him kick and punch wasn't worth writing a report about. Luke Whitman said he had spent the whole weekend glued to a kung fu movie marathon on TV, and he was up to his nostrils with martial arts. (When it comes to Luke Whitman, friends, it's all about the nose.) Chelsea Byrd said she was too nervous about her presentation to take any time off. Felipe Aguilar was being picked up early for a dentist appointment, and Mr Rock felt that Brandon Clarke was just a little too hyper that day to be able to sit still for the match.

So Zoe and I were the only ones to go into the gym for the matches, which was fine with me. I mean, who wants Luke "The Nose Tap" Whitman sitting within wiping distance of your shirtsleeve, anyway?

Ashley and Frankie were really glad to see us. Ashley looked great. She had decorated the back of her gi with a rhinestone map of Korea, to honour the country where Tae Kwon Do had first been developed.

"Hello, Mr Zipzer," Mr Love said. "And who is your *chapeau*-wearing friend?"

"This is Zoe McKelty from PS 9," I said proudly.

"I'm here at PS 87 to work on improving my reading and tracking skills," Zoe said to him. I looked at her in amazement. Imagine, just announcing a thing like that to a gi-wearing head teacher and a room of students you don't even know. That takes some kind of courage.

"Is it OK if we watch the matches?" I asked Mr Love.

It wasn't an automatic yes like I thought it would be. Mr Love rubbed his face thoughtfully. As he rubbed, I saw his index finger accidentally flick the Statue of Liberty mole that lives on his cheek. The more he rubbed his face, the more he flicked her, first in the arm part, then in the feet part, then in the butt part. She didn't seem to mind, though. She just hung onto his cheek welcoming all the tired and poor and huddled masses to America, just like the real Statue of Liberty does in the New York Harbor.

"If I let you stay, I want you to understand that this isn't a sporting match you're watching," Mr Love said. "Do you understand that?"

"Absolutely, Sir." I nodded.

"Tae Kwon Do is a combination of sport, self-defence and philosophy. You are watching a belief system in action, discipline in motion. Is that clear?"

"Crystal, Sir." I nodded harder this time, although I have to confess, he was losing me a little on the belief-system part.

"There will be no cheering for winners," he went on. "We are not here to win, are we, Mr Zipzer?"

"No, Sir. We are here to lose."

"Incorrect, Mr Zipzer. We are here neither to win nor to lose."

"Right you are, Sir. We're here to tie."

"Incorrect again, Mr Zipzer. We are not here to win or lose or tie, but to learn, to study with the master *sensei*, which in this case, would be me. Is that clear, Mr Zipzer?"

"Double crystal, Sir, with a big fat red cherry on top."

"In that case, you and your *chapeau*-wearing friend may stay. Are you *junbi*?"

"Uh ... *junbi*, Sir?"

"It means 'ready' in Korean."

"Oh. You bet, Sir. We're both *junbi*, aren't we, Zoe?"

"I'm as *junbi* as I'll ever be," she said with a giggle.

I could see that Frankie and Ashley were dying to burst out laughing, but they didn't dare. Mr Love was already walking into the middle of the ring, his Velcro shoes squeaking up a storm as he went.

"We'll begin with a women's match," he said. "Ashley Wong and Joelle Atkins, come forward, please."

Ashley walked into the middle of the ring, but there was no sign of Joelle. I looked around for her. I couldn't see her, but I could hear her voice coming from the general direction of Nick McKelty.

"Can you believe it?" I heard her whispering. "She wore a charm bracelet with penguins on it.

I mean, who does that? It's so incredibly second grade."

"Ms Atkins," Mr Love boomed in his extra loud voice. Joelle peeked out from behind the hugeness of Nick McKelty. Sure enough, her mobile phone was attached to her ear, and she was chattering away.

"Oops. Got to go," she said into the phone when she saw Mr Love staring her down. "Oodles of toodles."

"I'll take that," Mr Love said, holding out his hand for Joelle's phone. "You may pick it up on your way out."

It must have been painful for Joelle to hand over her mobile phone. I mean, that thing is like her third arm.

"Mrs Crock will help the girls into their *hogu*," Mr Love said. Mrs Crock, a nice woman who works in the attendance office, was holding two dark blue mats that looked like the chest protectors that catchers wear in baseball. She went over to Ashley and slipped one over her gi so that it covered most of her middle part.

"This *hogu* will serve as both protection for you and as a scoring target," Mr Love said.

"No way," squeaked Joelle. "I'm not wearing

that thing. It's so not in fashion."

"If you want to compete, then you will wear it," Mr Love said.

Mrs Crock slipped the *hogu* over Joelle's gi, but you would have thought she was covering her in bird poo.

"Eeuuww, this is gross," Joelle said. "Eeuuww, eeuuww, eeuuww."

"She is so ridiculously girly," Zoe whispered to me.

"If you think so now, wait until you see her moves," I whispered back. Ashley had told me that when Joelle did Tae Kwon Do, all she worried about was that she was going to break a fingernail.

Mr Love insisted that the two girls put on headgear and shin guards too. Then he positioned them in the centre of the ring so they were facing each other.

"When your opponent touches your *hogu* with a hand or a foot, she scores a point," he explained to them. "Of course, we are going to pull our punches and kicks, so as not to hurt the other person."

"You mean they don't get to punch and kick really hard?" Zoe whispered.

"Of course not," I said. "We're in school, after all."

"If you fall down or are taken down, your opponent scores another point," Mr Love went on. "The first person to score three points will be declared victorious."

Before then, I had no idea how a Tae Kwon Do sparring match was run. This was turning out to be really interesting and fun.

With their *hogu* and headgear and shin guards on, I could barely tell which girl was which. Thank goodness for the rhinestone map of Korea. That would be a surefire way to identify Ashley.

"Are you both *junbi*?" Mr Love asked.

"*Junbi*," Ashley answered.

"Whatever," Joelle said.

With that, Mr Love blew a whistle. Three short blasts and the match was on!

CHAPTER 22

*FIVE THINGS THAT JOELLE ATKINS SAID
DURING HER MATCH WITH ASHLEY*

1. Enough!
2. Enough!!
3. Enough!!!!!
4. Enough, I said!!!!!!!!!!!
5. I quit!

CHAPTER 23

I'M TELLING YOU, Ashley Wong was dynamite in the ring.

She whizzed around Joelle at lightning speed, spinning and twirling and leaping in the air like a gazelle. (To be honest, I'm not totally sure what a gazelle is, but I'm pretty sure it's some kind of leaping animal.) I don't know where she learned those moves, but Ashley had an impressive front kick, a pretty good side kick, a jumping strike, a forward strike and a reverse strike. In thirty seconds, she must have touched Joelle's *hogu* five times.

Joelle was not happy *at all*. She just stood there in the ring, clutching her *hogu* to her body with her pretty pink fingernails.

From the sidelines, Nick McKelty was shouting, "Move, Joelle! Let her have it!"

But Joelle didn't even so much as pick up a foot until she hollered, "I quit!" and stomped out of the ring.

Ashley was smiling like someone in a toothpaste commercial when the match was over. Zoe and I both wanted to stand up and cheer for her, but Mr Love had strictly forbidden it. Instead, I just gave her a huge thumbs-up and Zoe blew her a kiss. You have to admit, that was a pretty cute thing to do.

"This was an excellent display of Tae Kwon Do," Mr Love said to Ashley. "You show great promise when it comes to promising to become a very promising martial arts type person."

"Thanks," Ashley said. "I think."

"Next we will have a men's match," Mr Love said. "Will Frankie Townsend and Nick McKelty please come forward?"

Frankie got up and quietly took his place in the centre of the ring. Frankie is very humble about his athletic skills. You never hear him bragging about how great he is. He just gets the job done. Nick McKelty is totally the opposite. All he does is brag, with not much to back it up. As Papa Pete says, he's all Flash and no Gordon.

As McKelty walked into the ring, he pumped his fists above his head and took bows as if there were a real crowd cheering for him.

140

Hey, Nick, I wanted to shout. *This isn't the World Wrestling Federation.*

"Let's hear it for the champ," he said as he jogged up alongside Frankie. "I'm going to crush you, Townsend."

Mr Love wasn't impressed.

"Did you hear my introduction about Tae Kwon Do?" he asked Nick. "We are not here to defeat the enemy, but to defend ourselves."

"Bring it on," McKelty said. "I'm totally ready or as you like to say, I'm totally *junbi*."

"Mrs Crock will help you boys assemble your protective gear," Mr Love said. He reached into his pocket to pull out a small scorecard and a pencil.

"That cousin of yours is really something," I whispered to Zoe while Frankie was getting ready.

"I know he can be irritating," Zoe said, "but inside, he's just a big softie."

Actually, I didn't agree with her at all. I think that inside, Nick McKelty is a big bully. But one of the nice things about Zoe is that she has something good to say about everyone, so I decided not to argue with her about McKelty's insides.

141

Mrs Crock was having a hard time with Nick's *hogu*. She had to adjust the straps to make room for his tree trunk of a body.

"Stop wiggling around, Nick," she said. "And keep your arms still, please."

Mr Love and the other kids were busy straightening up the floor mats from the first match. As I watched McKelty getting ready, I thought I saw him take something out of his gi pocket and stuff it into his mouth. It looked like a chocolate Ding Dong.

What was he doing eating a Ding Dong at a moment like this? Could he be that hungry? No, not possible.

I decided that I had seen wrong.

"Are you *junbi*, gentlemen?" Mr Love asked when Mrs Crock had finished with McKelty's *hogu*.

"Yes, *sensei*," Frankie said. He bowed his head towards Nick, like you're supposed to do in the martial arts, to honour your opponent. McKelty didn't bow, which was so typical of him.

Mr Love blew the whistle, three short blasts, and both guys went into action.

Their styles couldn't have been more opposite. Frankie was all speed and grace, like a quarterback. McKelty was all power and force, like a linebacker.

It was actually a pretty good match. Frankie jumped in the air and did a spinning kick, touching McKelty's *hogu* with the tip of his toes.

Go, Frankie!

"One point for Townsend," Mr Love said, taking out his pencil to mark the scorecard.

Frankie started to do another spin but McKelty intercepted it by sticking his chunky arm into Frankie's path. His arm just happened to land on Frankie's *hogu*.

"One point for McKelty," Mr Love said, marking his scorecard.

When he saw that sticking his arm out was working, McKelty did it again. This time, Frankie blocked it. Then he spun around in the air, turned his back on McKelty and delivered an awesome reverse kick, landing his foot dead centre on McKelty's chest.

"Another point for Townsend," Mr Love said, looking down at the scorecard he was holding in his hand. It looked like his pencil point had broken, and he reached into his gi pocket for another pencil. Zoe looked over at Ashley and they gave each other a big smile. They were both enjoying the match.

That's how, in the split second when no one was looking, I saw something that no one else in the gym saw.

McKelty got right in Frankie's face and opened his mouth really wide, showing his tongue covered with goopy, half-chewed chocolate Ding Dong. Frankie couldn't believe what he was seeing. It was completely unexpected. I mean, who does that kind of thing during a martial arts competition?

For a second, Frankie just stood there, staring into McKelty's yucky mouth.

It was only a second, but one that McKelty used to his advantage. He reached out and threw a strike at Frankie's *hogu*, and when Frankie spun around to block it, McKelty stuck his foot out and tripped him up.

I couldn't believe what I was seeing. Frankie flew into the air, then landed with a thud on the mat. He was down!

"Two points for McKelty," Mr Love said, looking up from his scorecard. "One for the touch, one for the fall. That's three points to one. Match to McKelty."

I was on my feet in no time.

"Hey, that's not fair!" I hollered.

"Mr Zipzer," Mr Love said, "I appreciate your loyalty to your friend, but as you can see, Mr McKelty just scored one point for the strike and one point for the takedown, bringing his score to a match-winning three."

"But McKelty tricked him!" I said.

"He didn't do anything," Zoe whispered to me.

"Are you making an accusation, Mr Zipzer?" Mr Love asked.

"You bet I am! McKelty made Frankie look at his chocolatey disgusting Ding-Donged-up tongue!"

"Hank," Zoe said. "What are you talking about?"

"Check it out for yourself," I said. "Go ahead, McKelty. Show them what's in your mouth."

"Nothing," McKelty said. "I got nothing in my mouth. Where would I get a Ding Dong here in the gym, anyway?"

McKelty opened his mouth. I couldn't believe it. He had swallowed the whole chocolatey mess, and now there was no sign of it.

"But I saw you pop in that Ding Dong," I

said. "Didn't anyone else see that?"

No one answered, but I could see Zoe looking at me like I had lost my mind.

"I saw it," Frankie said.

"Of course, you'll say anything," McKelty said to him, "just to win."

That did it for me. Frankie Townsend was no cheater.

"There's got to be a wrapper in there," I said, pointing to McKelty's gi pocket. McKelty reached down and turned his pockets inside out. There was nothing in there.

"What about in his rucksack?"

"Mr Zipzer," Mr Love said. "I'm going to have to demand that you sit down. Mr McKelty won the match fair and square. Besides, as I said before, this is not about winning and losing. This is about discipline, and you are showing a tremendous lack of discipline."

"And you're behaving like a real jerk," Zoe whispered to me.

"It's not fair," I repeated.

"Since you persist with this line of accusation, I'm afraid I have to ask you to leave the gym right now," Mr Love said.

"You cheated," I said to McKelty.

"You're a sore loser," McKelty answered.

Frankie wasn't saying anything. I think he knew that arguing would just make him look like a sore loser too.

"Fine," I said. "I'm leaving. Come on, Zoe. Let's go."

I got up to go, but Zoe didn't.

"Come on, Zoe. Let's go back to Reading Gym. Aren't you coming?"

"No, Hank. I'm not," she said.

It was then I noticed that Zoe had tears in her eyes.

CHAPTER 24

I WENT BACK to the Reading Gym and tried to work on my scrapbook, but I couldn't concentrate on anything. I was steaming mad. Mr Rock didn't notice because he was giving special attention to Chelsea Byrd. She's a very shy girl and she'd been extra special nervous about having to present her autobiography to the class the next week. Mr Rock was helping her review it.

As I sat there looking around the library, a million questions raced around in my brain. Why hadn't Zoe come with me? Why was she crying? Why couldn't she understand that her cousin was a cheater? Wait a minute ... why was Luke Whitman blowing his nose on a piece of yellow construction paper?

A few minutes later, when the class was over, I dashed across the hall and waited for Zoe outside the gym. She was the first to come out, since the kids in the Tae Kwon Do class had to stay after to put the floor mats away.

She walked right past me.

"Hey, Zoe, wait up," I called.

"I'm not speaking to you," she said.

"Why? What'd I do?"

"You made up that awful story about Nick just because you wanted Frankie to win."

"I didn't make anything up! Nick really did eat that Ding Dong," I said. "And he did stick his tongue out at Frankie. I saw it with my own two eyes."

"Oh, really, Hank? I didn't see it. Ashley didn't see it. Mr Love didn't see it. Explain that."

"Because you and Ashley were busy waving and saying hi and stuff," I answered. "And Mr Love was keeping score."

"There was no wrapper, Hank. Nothing in Nick's pocket."

"So what? That doesn't prove anything. Plus Frankie saw it too."

We had reached the door of the library.

"I'm going inside to get my stuff now," Zoe said. "When I come out, I'd like you not to be here."

"But..."

I had no chance to finish the sentence, because

she turned and went into the library. I stood at the door, gathering my thoughts up, as much as I can ever gather my thoughts up, that is. Then I followed her in. She was already talking with Chelsea Byrd.

"You'll do fine," I heard her saying to Chelsea. "Everyone gets nervous, but we're all here to support you."

"Psst, Zoe," I whispered.

But she didn't even look my way.

I ran out into the hall and stopped Frankie and Ashley as they were coming out of the gym.

"Frankie, you've got to help me," I said. "Zoe thinks I made up the thing about the Ding Dong. You've got to tell her it's true."

"Drop it, Zip," Frankie said.

"You mean you're not going to say anything about what happened?"

"Tae Kwon Do is not about winning and losing," Frankie said. "McKelty knows what he did. He's got to deal with that."

Frankie started walking down the hall.

"So you're just going to let McKelty pull a fast one like that?"

He stopped and looked hard at me.

"Listen, Zip, the one thing I've learned about

150

sports is that you get all kinds of calls. Some are good calls. Some are bad calls. And the deal is, you can't complain about them or you just look like a chump. So let's forget about this, OK?"

"No, not OK. Listen, Frankie … I need you to tell Zoe that I wasn't making this up. She thinks I'm lying about it."

"You have to admit, Zip, you're getting a little confused about what's true and what isn't these days. Like the deal with not telling your dad about Reading Gym. Come on, dude. You should tell him."

"That's easy for you to say. You don't have to live with him."

"Yeah, but you do, and lying to him isn't going to make it any easier."

"So you're not going to back me up with Zoe?"

"I'm done with covering for you, dude."

I turned to Ashley.

"Did you see the Ding Dong?" I asked her. "Even a little tiny piece of it? One or two crumbs, maybe?"

"I didn't, Hank. I'm really sorry," she said.

As Ashley hurried to catch up with Frankie, I just stood there fuming. To make matters worse,

Nick the Tick picked that very moment to walk out of the gym.

"Told you I'd take your pal down," he said with a grin.

"You cheated," I said to him.

"You got no proof, Sherlock. So it looks like I'm the winner and you and your pal are the losers."

Call me immature, but I actually growled at McKelty. I didn't plan to do it, but it just sort of fell out of my mouth before I could stop it. A real growl, like a lion or a tiger.

"Yeah, like you scare me," McKelty laughed as he walked off. "So long, Zipper Boy."

As if to prove that the day couldn't have got any worse, Mr Love grabbed me on his way out and asked me to help him carry his stuff back to his office. Out of the corner of my eye, I saw Zoe leaving the library with Chelsea. But me, I was stuck squeaking down the hall next to Mr Love, toting his gym bag in one hand and his snowman scarf in the other.

Now if that's not a terrible way to end a terrible day, I don't know what is.

CHAPTER 25

I TRIED CALLING ZOE the minute I got home, but her mum said she wasn't feeling well and couldn't come to the phone.

I tried calling her the next day when I got home, but I just got their voicemail. It was her voice saying, "Leave your name, message and favourite song after the beep."

"Name: Hank Improvement Zipzer," I said. "Message: I'd like to talk to Zoe. Favourite Song: 'Wheels on the Bus'."

I hoped she'd be impressed by my cute message and call back.

But she didn't call back.

I waited for her in our booth at McKelty's Roll 'N' Bowl on Thursday after school.

She didn't show up.

But Nick the Tick did. With Joelle "The Phone Fanatic" Atkins by his side.

"If you're waiting for Zoe, you're going to

be waiting a long time," McKelty said. "Like forever."

"How would you know, McKelty?"

"Well, she told us she thinks you acted like a bad sport and a poor loser," Joelle said.

"And then she told me she doesn't like you any more, not even a little bit," McKelty added.

"She didn't really say that part, did she?" I asked, trying to stop my voice from quivering.

"Text her yourself," Joelle said, offering me her mobile phone. "Ask her."

I think you know by now that I'm not a big spelling guy, which also means I'm not a big texting guy. I see all those letters on that little keypad, and my eyes just start to spin in their sockets.

"That's OK," I said to Joelle. "I'll text her later."

"He probably doesn't know how," McKelty said, which may have been the first true thing he's ever said.

"I'll text her for you," Joelle said.

That was the last thing I wanted, to have Joelle in the middle of my private conversation with Zoe. She'd be announcing what we said from the top of the Empire State Building.

"No, thanks," I said. "I'm not really in the mood to text right now. I'm an after-dinner texting kind of guy, not an afternoon texting kind of guy."

"Wow," said Joelle. "You have special times of the day when you text?"

"Doesn't everyone?" I answered. "I instant message in the morning, e-mail in the afternoon, text after dinner. If I don't keep them separate, I'm just communicating non-stop all day long, and you know what that does."

"What?" asked Joelle, looking alarmed.

"Rots the brain," I whispered to her. "Next thing you know, you're wearing a bracelet with penguins on it and thinking that's OK."

I saw Joelle gasp, then fold up her phone and put it in her pocket.

At dinner that night, I was so sad I could hardly eat. Cheerio could tell something was wrong. He sprawled out on top of my feet and nuzzled my ankles. It's his little dachshund way of showing support.

"What's wrong, honey?" my mum asked. "You look like you lost your best friend."

"I did," I said. "Zoe and I had a fight."

"It must be in the air," Emily said. "Robert

and I had a fight too. We're not speaking."

"What was your fight about?" I asked her.

"Robert said that chickens can't fly, and I told him that's not entirely true because the longest recorded flight of a chicken is thirteen seconds. Then he said that's not really flying, and I said, tell that to the chicken who stayed in the air for thirteen seconds."

"Wow," I said. "You guys get pretty upset over poultry."

"It wasn't about the chickens. He was acting like a know-it-all," my know-it-all sister said. "What did you and Zoe fight about?"

I didn't want to go into it with Emily. I mean, there are some things a fourth-grader can't understand. They're still fighting about flying chickens and stuff. Not like us fifth-graders who fight about real human-type things.

"We fought about ducks," I said. "I said that a duck's quack doesn't echo, and she said it does."

"Well, she's right," my dad piped up, putting his glasses on top of his head and taking a break from our beet and mushroom casserole. "Many people believe that a duck's quack does not echo. In reality, the quack has a particular sound quality that makes it difficult to hear the echo, but it actually does echo."

"Wow, Dad. That's really … um … interesting."

"All knowledge is interesting, Hank. That's what I keep trying to tell you. You should call Zoe and apologize."

Like the way I should apologize to you for not telling the truth, I thought to myself.

Ever since Frankie had that talk with me, I had tried to find the right moment to tell my dad the truth about the Reading Gym. But trust me, that is not an easy thing to do, and I was still working on getting up the courage.

Fortunately, the doorbell rang, taking my mind off everything. I got up to answer it. It was Robert, standing at the door holding a bunch of half-wilted flowers.

"It's Robert," I called out. "Should I let him in?"

Emily jumped up and ran to the door.

"I came to apologize," Robert said, handing Emily the bunch of flowers. "I wasn't being a good listener. You know a great deal about chicken flight, and I respect that about you."

"Oh, Robert." Emily sighed.

"Here, you better take these fast," Robert

said, offering Emily the flowers. "The pollen makes my allergies flare up. I can feel my nose starting to drip already."

Robert sneezed a big wet sneeze. Any normal person would have slammed the door in his face. But not our Emily. She opened the door wider, grabbed the flowers and smiled a dopey little smile.

"Do you want to come in?" she asked Robert. "I have some reptile drawings we can colour. And a new box of fruit-scented markers."

"Sounds like fun," Robert said.

I watched them skip off to the kitchen table, take the caps off Emily's new markers and start sniffing them.

Boy, oh boy, did I ever wish Zoe and I were back in the fourth grade, when a couple of pineapple- and grape-scented markers and some reptile drawings could solve everything.

CHAPTER 26

THAT WEEKEND, the only thing that interested me even a little bit was working on my life-story scrapbook. Not to be all goopy or anything, but I think I liked working on it because the scrapbook reminded me of Zoe and the fun we'd had working on our autobiographies together.

On Sunday, while waiting for Zoe to call (which she didn't), I practised my presentation in the clubhouse for Ashley and Frankie. At first, Frankie didn't want to come because he was still mad at me. Well, not so much mad as frustrated. He said he just wanted me to set things right. But Ashley talked him into coming, and I'm so glad she did. We had a good time remembering all the things I put in there – like our first day of pre-school when Alan Kaufman tried to run me over with a toy fire truck and Frankie had to defend me, or the day Ashley and I tried to make egg rolls by rolling eggs on the kitchen floor. Boy, did we make a mess!

By the time I was done presenting my scrapbook, we were all laughing like always. We've had too much fun to let anything serious ever come between us.

The amazing thing was that I was very comfortable reading the scrapbook out loud. I didn't stumble over very many words at all, and I was able to read with real expression. That was a first for me.

"I want to come and see your presentation," Ashley said.

"We should be there, Ash," Frankie said. "We're the co-stars."

"It's on Tuesday," I told them, "which means you'll have to miss Tae Kwon Do."

"I'll take it up with Mr Love," Frankie said. "Got anything to offer him, Ashweena?"

"I could offer to put rhinestones on one of his snowman scarves," she suggested.

"Outstanding idea," Frankie said with a nod. "The way to Mr Love's heart is through his snowmen."

It turns out it was easy for Frankie and Ashley to get out of going to Tae Kwon Do. On that Tuesday, Mrs Crock came on the loudspeaker after lunch to announce that Mr Love had slipped on the cafeteria floor when one of the Velcro straps of his tennis shoes came loose. He had gone home to sit on a heating pad. Anyone in his Tae Kwon Do class could either have their parents pick them up early or go to Mr Rock's Reading Gym or Ms Woolsey's knitting club.

After school, we all went to the Reading Gym together. As we walked in, I saw Zoe sitting in the front row, next to Chelsea Byrd.

"Hi, Zoe," we all said almost in unison.

"Hi, Frankie. Hi, Ashley," she said.

Wow. It was so bad I couldn't even get a "hi."

Poor Chelsea. She looked like she was going to throw up.

"Hi, Chelsea," I said. "You look nice today."

"Thanks, Hank." She gave me a nervous smile. I glanced over at Zoe, as if to say, "At least somebody is being nice to me."

Frankie, Ashley and I took our seats in the second row, behind Chelsea and Zoe, just as Mr Rock came to the front of the class.

"Hi, kids," he said. "Big day today. I'm really looking forward to each of you sharing your life story. I've put all your names in this fine New York Mets hat I happen to have. Chelsea, why

161

don't you come up and help me draw the names to establish what order we'll go in."

Let me just point out two things here about what a cool guy Mr Rock is. First of all, he's a Mets fan, like I always knew he would be. And second of all, he knew Chelsea was nervous so he picked her to come up and draw the names. That's what I call being a decent dude.

As Chelsea picked the names from the hat, Mr Rock read each one out loud.

"OK, first at bat will be Zoe McKelty," he said. "Then Chelsea Byrd, followed by Hank Zipzer, with Luke Whitman batting clean-up." (Now if Luke would just clean up his nose, everything would be great.)

I could see Chelsea swallowing hard. She really didn't want to do this.

"The bottom of the line-up," Mr Rock went on, "features none other than Kacey Wilson, followed by Felipe Aguilar, Sloane Wilson and Brandon Clarke. Did I leave anyone out?"

"Yeah, the coolest guy here," came a voice from the door.

There was only one voice that loud and obnoxious, and you guessed it, it belonged to Nick the Tick McKelty.

"Are you joining us, Nick?" Mr Rock asked.

"Yeah," Nick answered, coming in and taking the seat next to me. "My dad can't get here... I think he's in Washington DC, visiting the president. Anyway, I'm stuck here until Mr Love recovers from his sore rump."

"Well, sit down and put your rucksack under your chair," Mr Rock told him. "We're about to get started with our presentations and we need the utmost courtesy from our visitors."

"You don't have to worry about me," McKelty said. "I am Mr Courtesy."

Right, and I am Mr Brainiac.

McKelty sprawled out in the seat next to me.

"How you doing, Zipper Dork?" he whispered.

By that time, Zoe had taken her place at the front of the room. She was setting up a mini boom box that had her music recorded. She had taken the drumsticks out of her back pocket and put them on the table in front of her. When everything was ready, she took a deep breath, picked up her paper and pressed play on her boombox. The sound of her singing "The Wheels on the Bus" filled the room.

"Even as a baby, I always loved music," she

163

read. "The first song I can remember hearing was 'The Wheels on the Bus'." As the song played, she picked up her drumsticks and tapped out a rhythm on the table. It sounded great, like people's footsteps marching in time to the turning of the wheels.

She continued reading her paper, alternating her words with her favourite songs. She accompanied each song on the drumsticks. A few times when she was reading, she lost her place and had to stop, but she didn't let that fluster her.

"Give me a minute to find my place, guys," she said the first time it happened. "I have tracking problems and sometimes I can't follow the words and I mess up totally."

I looked over at Mr Rock and could see him smile at that. He's always telling us that we should let people know if we're having difficulty reading something, that there's nothing to be ashamed of. I can tell you from personal experience, that sounds easy but it's really hard to do. You just keep waiting for someone to make fun of you.

My eyes stayed glued on Zoe, just like they did the very first time I ever saw her. I was so sorry that she didn't like me any more, because

I sure liked her. She was interesting through and through.

"So now I'm in fifth grade," she said, coming to the end of her presentation. "I love music, dancing, my family, my cat Bill, wearing hats and playing the drums I'll end now with a little drum solo I made up myself."

Then she turned her newsboy cap around so the front was in the back and played a really rocking beat on the tabletop, ending with a rat-a-tat-tat on the bottom of the metal wastebasket.

Everyone applauded. Mr Rock put his fingers in his mouth and whistled loudly. I clapped so hard I thought my hands were going to fall off.

Zoe smiled, and even glanced over at me. That felt good.

"That's the way us McKeltys do it!" Nick cheered as though he had ever done anything half as well as that.

Zoe slid into her seat in front of me.

"You did great," I whispered to her. "I knew you would."

Zoe didn't answer. Her eyes looked a little sad, though, as if to say, "I'm really sorry we're not friends any more, Hank."

"Next up is Chelsea Byrd," Mr Rock said.

Chelsea stood up and went to the front of the class. She took out a bottle of water she had brought from home, opened it and put it next to her on the table.

"I'm pretty nervous," she said in a small voice for such a tall girl. She's only in the fifth grade, but she towers over all the boys in our class. I hope she's got a sky hook, because she could do some serious damage on the basketball court.

You could just feel the tension pouring out of Chelsea. Her hands were even shaking a little as she took a sip from her water bottle, picked up her scrapbook and faced the group.

"Begin whenever you're ready," Mr Rock said to her. "There's nothing to worry about. We're all here to make this easy for you, aren't we?"

Everyone nodded yes. Everyone but one person.

And I think we all know who that one person was.

CHAPTER 27

CHELSEA CLEARED HER THROAT, took another swig from her water bottle and began.

"This is a picture of me on the day I was born," she said, pointing to a photo on the first page of her scrapbook. "The caption I wrote says, '*Hi World! I'm here and I'm bald.*'"

Everyone laughed. First of all, that was a pretty funny thing to say. And second of all, we were trying to make Chelsea comfortable.

I didn't hear McKelty laughing, which is unusual, because when he laughs it sounds like a foghorn going off. I glanced over at him and saw him reaching down and fumbling in his rucksack for something. It was just like him not to pay attention.

Chelsea turned the page and held up her scrapbook so we could all see.

"This is a picture of my first birthday party," she said. "I'm the one with chocolate cake all over my face. The caption says, '*There really is a face behind all the chocolate frosting, I promise.*'"

The picture made me think of my first birthday party. I don't remember it, of course, but we have a picture of it in our family album. Papa Pete is holding out a dill pickle and I'm sitting in a high chair, taking a lick of it and looking like I'm going to cry. Things change, because I'm a huge dill pickle fan now. Next to pepperoni pizza and black-and-white cookies, they're my favourite food.

"I love chocolate," McKelty blurted out as if anyone cared.

"Nick, this is Chelsea's turn to talk," Mr Rock said.

McKelty's interruption rattled Chelsea a little, and as she went to turn the page, she dropped her scrapbook on the floor.

"Butterfingers," McKelty said, in a whisper loud enough for everyone to hear.

Mr Rock went immediately to the front of the room to help Chelsea pick up her scrapbook and reopen it to the right page. While that was happening, I shot McKelty a dirty look, trying to send him a message that no one appreciated him interrupting Chelsea. He didn't see me, though, because he was busy slipping something into his jacket pocket. I couldn't see what it was.

"Go on, Chelsea," Mr Rock said. "You're doing great."

Chelsea picked up her water and took another gulp.

"When I was three," she went on, swallowing hard, "I had to go to the hospital to get stitches because I got my finger caught in a door. I was very scared, but a nice doctor took a rubber glove and blew it up like a balloon and gave it to me. This is me at the hospital. The caption says, '*What an unusual balloon. It has five fingers!*'"

It was a little hard for me to hear Chelsea reading the caption, because McKelty was making noise as usual. I don't know what he was doing in his pocket, but it sounded like he was crinkling up paper or something. Knowing him, he was probably destroying a spelling test he got a zero on.

"Excellent, Chelsea," Mr Rock said. "'Unusual' is a very difficult word to read. Go on!"

I think Chelsea was starting to relax a little. I could see that her hands weren't shaking as much as she turned to the next page.

"This page isn't a picture," she said. "It's a copy of my favourite poem that my mum used to read to me every night. It's called *The Owl and the Pussycat*."

"Sounds stupid," McKelty muttered.

I turned around to tell him to be quiet, but he already had his back to me. He was still fidgeting with something in his pocket.

"Why don't you try to read us a little of the poem," Mr Rock said.

"It's pretty hard," Chelsea answered.

"Just give it a try," Mr Rock said. "We're all interested, aren't we, kids?"

Everyone nodded.

Chelsea took some water and a deep breath, and then slowly started to read, pausing a lot between the words to try to figure them out. It sounded like me reading. I knew how nervous she must have been. Every time I have to read out loud, my stomach feels all jimbly and jambly.

"The owl and the pussycat went to sea in a beau ... beau ... beautiful pea-green boat," Chelsea read.

She looked up and could see from our faces that we were all rooting for her. She smiled a little. I felt really happy for her and flashed her my best Hank Zipzer grin. As she smiled back, her eyes drifted to the chair next to me. Suddenly, her expression changed. She looked scared or disturbed or something and cast her eyes back down on her scrapbook really fast. I whipped around to look at McKelty. His cheeks looked very puffy, like there was something in his mouth.

"You're not doing the tongue thing again, are you, McKelty?" I whispered to him.

"Hank, no talking now," Mr Rock said. "Chelsea needs our full attention while she's reading her poem."

I pretended to look at Chelsea, but I kept one eye on McKelty while Chelsea went on reading her poem.

"They took some honey and plenty of money wrapped up in a five-pound note," she read. "The owl looked up to the stars above and sang to a small guitar..."

With that, Chelsea looked up, pretending to be the singing owl. In that one little glance, there was time for her eyes to catch a glimpse of Nick McKelty. And in that split second, the big lug opened his mouth and stuck out his tongue. It was covered with chocolate goop and chunky chocolate crumbs.

Oh no! It was another Ding Dong attack! And once again, no one saw it but me. Me and Chelsea Byrd.

Chelsea gasped and dropped the scrapbook. On its way down to the ground, it nicked the table and knocked over her bottle of water. The scrapbook she had worked so hard on landed *kerplop* on the floor. The water gushed out of the bottle and spilled all over everything, dripping onto the floor like pouring rain. I could see the ink on the pages turning into a blue river as the water washed over her handwritten captions.

Chelsea burst into tears. Mr Rock was next to her in no time.

"It's OK, Chelsea," he said, picking up her scrapbook and blotting it with his handkerchief. "Accidents happen. That's why we call them accidents."

"That was no accident," I shouted out.

Everyone turned to stare at me.

"McKelty Ding-Donged her!" I said.

Zoe whipped her head round and gave me an angry stare. "You're not starting this again, are you, Hank?" she whispered.

"You didn't see what happened," I whispered back. "I did!"

"What are you talking about, Hank?" Mr Rock asked.

"He stuck his chocolatey tongue out at Chelsea," I said. "I saw him do it. And it threw her off completely."

"Is this true, Chelsea?" Mr Rock said. "Did Nick stick his tongue out at you?"

Chelsea was so embarrassed that she wouldn't even lift up her head to answer. She just buried her face in her hands and cried.

"Nick, did you do such a thing?" Mr Rock asked him.

"There's nothing in my mouth, Mr Rock," Nick said. "See?"

He opened his mouth, and just like at the Tae Kwon Do match, it was empty.

"Look in his pocket," I said. "I saw him take the Ding Dong from his rucksack and slip it into his pocket. I bet there's a wrapper in there."

"Nick, can I see what's in your pocket?" Mr Rock asked.

Nick put his hand in his pocket and turned it inside out. There was nothing in there.

"The other pocket," I said. "He took it from the other pocket."

Mr Rock came over and stood next to Nick.

He gave him a look like I have never seen Mr Rock give anyone else before. It was strict. It was tough. It was disappointed.

"I'd like to see what's in the other pocket," Mr Rock said.

"Zipperbutt just makes stuff up," McKelty said.

"NOW!" Mr Rock said.

McKelty reached into his pocket and turned it inside out.

A short, stubby pencil fell out.

Then a little blue NERF ball.

Then a ChapStick.

The last thing to fall out was a crumpled up Ding Dong wrapper.

"I don't know where that came from," Nick McKelty said.

But I knew. And Frankie knew. And Mr Rock knew. And Chelsea knew.

And now, finally, Zoe knew too.

CHAPTER 28

MR ROCK BENT DOWN and picked the Ding Dong wrapper up off the floor. He pulled at his collar and loosened his tie, just like my dad does when he's really mad.

"Nick, I can't believe you would do something like this," he said.

"I was hungry," Nick said, "so I had a little snack. Can I help it if I'm a messy eater?"

"You intentionally tried to distract Chelsea," Mr Rock said. "That was wrong, Nick. Do you understand that?"

McKelty gave a "So what's the big deal?" kind of shrug. Even if he was feeling bad, he sure wasn't going to let Mr Rock see it.

"There will be consequences for this," Mr Rock said. "Severe consequences. For starters, I'm going to call your father right after class, even if he is hanging out with the President of the United States, which by the way, I doubt very much. And tomorrow, you're going to have a nice long visit with Mr Love. I think you'd better get used to the detention room, because you're going to be seeing a lot of it."

Chelsea was on her hands and knees, picking up the pages from her scrapbook and trying to shake the water off them.

"I don't think I can finish the presentation," she said to Mr Rock.

"Another time, Chelsea," Mr Rock said. "You've done a fine job, and I'm very happy to see how much your reading skills are improving."

Everyone gave Chelsea high fives as she took her seat in the front row.

"So, Hank, you're next," Mr Rock said as he perched on top of the desk McKelty was sitting in. I could tell he was going to keep a close eye on him. "Think you're OK to go on?"

I was more than OK. I was pumped up. I wanted to get up there and do the best presentation I'd ever done. I wanted McKelty to know that his bully tactics didn't work in the Reading Gym. I wanted to get even with him not just for me, but for Chelsea and everyone else who was too shy to stand up to him.

"You bet," I told Mr Rock.

"Teach that guy a thing or two," Ashley whispered as I went up to the front of the class.

"Yeah," Frankie agreed with Ashley. "You're the dude to do it."

I placed my scrapbook on the table and looked out over the class. Zoe was smack in the middle of the front row, and I could feel her eyes on me. Her turquoise eyes. "The presentation I had planned for today was to show all of you my life story scrapbook," I said. "Here it is. It's filled with lots of wonderful memories from my past. I've worked really hard on putting it together. But because of what just happened, I've changed my mind. I'd like to talk about another part of my life, one that it's not so easy to talk about."

Mr Rock stood up from his seat on the desk. He looked surprised and curious.

"For most of my life, I had learning differences and didn't even know it," I began. "I always knew that most subjects in school were hard for me. Spelling, maths, reading, handwriting. My best friends, Ashley and Frankie, sailed right through them with no problems. Me, I always had problems.

"Last year, after Dr Berger tested me, I found out that my problems were because I have real actual learning differences that make it hard for me to learn in the regular way. Finding this out was the biggest relief of my life. It was incredible to know that I wasn't stupid, I just learn differently."

Mr Rock was smiling at me. So were Ashley and Frankie. I didn't have the nerve to look at Zoe, because I didn't know how she was reacting. I just knew that I had to go on, to try to say what Chelsea Byrd couldn't say.

"Even though it's a relief to have a name for it, I think we all know that having learning differences isn't easy," I said. "I'm always aware that school is hard for me, that reading is hard for me, and that I'm not like everyone else. One of the most difficult things I can ever do is to stand in front of people and read out loud. The words jump around on the page. Any little sound or sight distracts me. I lose my place and can't find it. And then I feel so embarrassed I just want to find a cave and hide in it like a big grizzly bear."

"That's what just happened to me," Chelsea said.

"I know it is, Chelsea," I answered. "I bet it's happened to all of us in Reading Gym. We all know what it feels like."

Then I looked right at Nick McKelty.

"One thing I know for sure is that if you really and truly know what it feels like to be embarrassed about yourself, you'd never make someone else feel like that."

"You're the man, Hank," Brandon Clarke piped up, raising his fist in the air.

"The thing about us kids with learning differences is, we're just like everyone else in most ways," I said, walking over to Nick so I was standing right in front of him. "We're smart. We're funny. We're nice. We have lots of talents. And we don't want to feel bad about ourselves just because we need some extra help in school."

"You tell that dude!" Felipe Aguilar called out.

"Making fun of us is not OK," I said right to McKelty's face.

"Go, Hank!" Sloane Wilson called out.

"And making us feel bad about ourselves is not OK!"

"It sure isn't!" called out her sister Kacey.

"And being rude is not OK."

"You know it," shouted Luke Whitman, with both nostrils finger-free.

"And most of all, Nick McKelty, being a bully

and picking on people who you think are weak is definitely not OK. Not ever! Am I right, guys?"

Everyone in class jumped up on their feet and started to scream and yell and whistle and applaud.

But I only saw one person, the one who was applauding the loudest. And that was Zoe McKelty.

CHAPTER 29

MAYBE *I* ONLY SAW Zoe McKelty, but there was another person who saw me. Someone I hadn't counted on. Someone who showed up by surprise. And that someone was Stanley Zipzer. I don't know how long he had been standing in the doorway, but when I finished my presentation, he motioned for me to come to the door to speak with him.

"Dad," I said. "What are you doing here?"

He took my arm and guided me out into the hall.

"I ran into Frankie's mum in the lift, and she said she got a call from someone at school that Tae Kwon Do was canceled," he said. "So I volunteered to pick all of you up. But you weren't in that class, were you? From what I just heard, I gather you haven't been there for some time."

"I'm so sorry, Dad. I wanted to tell you that I had switched to the Reading Gym. But I know

181

it upsets you that I have learning differences and need to be in special classes, and I just couldn't bring myself to tell you."

"So you lied," he said.

I nodded.

"Lying is never the right thing to do. I hope you understand that, Hank. And I hope you'll never forget that."

I couldn't even look at him. I felt like a total jerk.

"That being said, I want you to know that I listened carefully to what you had to say in there. And I was proud of you. I understand how you feel now – how I've made you feel about having learning challenges. I'll try to do better. I promise."

"And I'll try not to lie to you, Dad," I said. "I promise."

He reached out and gave me a hug. It was a Stanley Zipzer hug, meaning it was quick and kind of embarrassing. But it was a hug, and I'll take it.

"Now go back inside to that girl with the hat who can't take her eyes off you," he said.

And I did. Happily.

CHAPTER 30

TEN GREAT THINGS THAT
HAPPENED THE VERY NEXT DAY

1. Nick McKelty got kicked out of Tae Kwon Do class for cheating and got two weeks of after-school detention.
2. Nick McKelty had to personally apologize to Chelsea Byrd.
3. Chelsea Byrd got an *A* on her Reading Gym presentation.
4. Hank Zipzer got an *A*-plus on his Reading Gym presentation (the first ever in his whole entire life).
5. Stanley Zipzer went to the bookshop and bought a book on how to raise kids with learning challenges.
6. Zoe McKelty asked Hank Zipzer to go and get a root beer.
7. Hank Zipzer sang Zoe McKelty his own

special super-duper version of "The Wheels on the Bus", and she laughed for five minutes straight.

8. Frankie Townsend was made junior *sensei* of the Tae Kwon Do class and was asked to demonstrate the moves that Mr Love's sore rump prevented him from doing.

9. Ashley Wong presented Mr Love with a scarf where all the snowmen had blue rhinestone eyes, and he made her the official rhinestoner of our school.

10. Nick McKelty lost his Ding Dong privileges indefinitely.

11. Zoe McKelty gave Hank Zipzer an envelope that said, "Do Not Open Until Valentine's Day."

Hank's Note: OK, so I listed eleven great things that happened, not ten. Give me a break, will you? It's me, Hank, and I have learning challenges, you know!

CHAPTER 31

I BET YOU'RE dying to know what was in Zoe's envelope.

Well, what do you *think* was in it? A valentine, of course.

I bet you're dying to know what the valentine said.

Well, sorry, friends. That's going to have to stay my little secret.

Hey, a guy is entitled to some privacy, you know.

What's that? You don't think that's fair?

OK, I'll give you a break.

If you're truly bursting with curiosity about what Zoe's valentine said, it's in the scrapbook that's included in this book. (Since I never got to present my scrapbook for the Reading Gym, I put it in this book so you can check it out.) You don't have to thank me. I'm glad to do it.

Hey, I wouldn't let you close this book if

you're truly bursting with curiosity. After all, I'm your pal, Hank. And I'm on your side.

You can count on it.

This is a scrapbook about the life of me, Hank Zipzer. When Mr Rock first told us that we had to write about our life, I thought that was a really great assignment because I have a lot to say about my life. Right away, I started to make a list of all the wonderful things that have happened to me. But then, I lost the list. At least, I think I lost the list because I thought I put it in the pocket of my Mets parka but when I went to look for it, all I found were lint balls, part of an old Snickers bar and a treat for Cheerio that had been in the shape of a dog bone but now looked like a fingernail.

I think you know that I'm not a person who'd let an empty pocket get in my way. So I made another list of all the cool things I wanted to put in the scrapbook and I put that list in a very safe place. The problem was, it was so safe, even I couldn't remember where it was.

After that, I figured the writing thing wasn't going to work out because I'm just not a write-things-down kind of guy. Instead, I got out a bottle of glue and some tape and scissors and I went to work pasting and taping scraps on paper. And guess what? Before you could say, "This is the life of me," I had the scrapbook done. And here it is.

I really love looking through it
because I feel like my
imagination has such personality.
I hope you agree.

So, here it is, The Life of Me.
Enter at your own risk!!

Hank

My First Poem

I'm a tube of toothpaste.
I make your teeth all white.
When Mummy says,
"Go in and brush!"
I always say, "All right!"

These are a couple of pages from my baby book, which is a book my mum kept with all kinds of embarrassing facts about me as a baby.

BABY'S FIRST TOOTH:
At seven months, Hank finally gets his first tooth. It's on the bottom row, and it's coming in sideways. Poor little guy. He keeps rubbing it and crying.

Who wouldn't cry? I mean, you're a little baby, just getting used to being alive, and suddenly, here comes this monster tooth poking through your gums. Ow!

BABY'S FIRST WORD:
Hank's first word is "uh-oh". Unless that's not really a word, in which case, his actual first word is "cookie".

Too bad I didn't know the baby-talk words for "black-and-white cookie", which is my very favourite and probably was back then too.

(I wrote my own notes next to her notes.)

BABY'S HOBBIES:

Hank likes to lie in his cot and stare up at the lightbulbs on the ceiling.

I know, I know. It's not much of a hobby, but what else is there to do when you can't talk, eat pickles or play video games?

BABY'S BEST FRIENDS:

Hank seems to like to play with Frankie Townsend and Ashley Wong, two other babies who live in our building.

What did I tell you? We've been best friends since forever.

The Day Emily Was Born

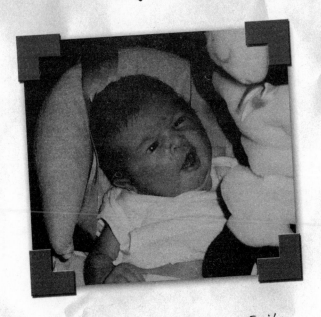

This is a picture of my sister, Emily, soon after she was born. I think she looks a lot like Katherine the iguana, except that Katherine is much better looking.

WELCOME HOME
EMILY!

Papa Pete made a "Welcome Home" banner
for Emily when they brought her home from
the hospital. I wanted it to say,
"Go back where you came from!"

This is a
birthday card I
made for Emily
when she was born.
It's impossible to
read, but I think it
says, "What's the
point of having a
birthday when you
can't even eat chocolate cake?"

Three Good Work Badges from Preschool

(This was when I was still good at school.)

Good Work, Hank!

For Washing Your Hands with Soap!

Good Work, Hank!

For Finishing All Your Raisins!

Good Work, Hank!

For Wearing a Fire Helmet Every Day This Week!

My First List
by Hank (age 5)

Ten Things I Do All Day

1. Play
2. Play
3. Play
4. Play
5. Play
6. Play
7. Play
8. Eat Graham crackers
9. Play
10. Poop

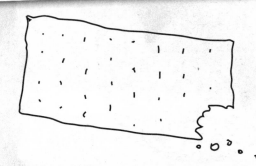

Cheerio came to join the Zipzer
family when I was five, and I wrote
a poem about him.

Cheerio

I have a dog named Cheerio
When I don't see him,
my eyes get all tear-i-o.

**PLEASE RESPECT
THE TREE GARDEN

CURB
YOUR DOG**

Our local no pooping sign. It's too bad
Cheerio can't read.

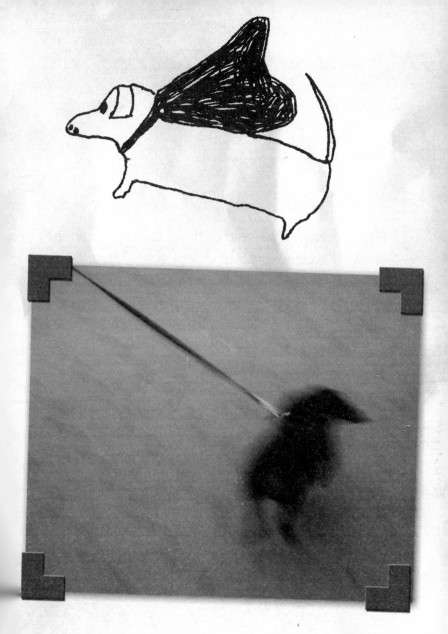

My dog Cheerio has super powers.
He runs so fast you can't even see his
cute little legs!

My Favourite Clothes List
by Hank Zipzer, age 5

When I was five years old, I made up a list
of my favourite clothes and told Papa Pete
to write it down. Then I gave the list to my
mum and said these were the only clothes
I would wear to school. She kept the list
tucked into the corner of the mirror in her
bedroom for a long time, but she gave it to
me to put in this scrapbook. Here it is.

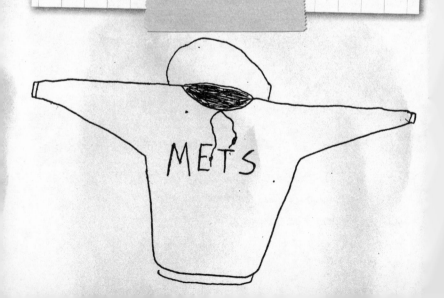

MET S

My Favourite Clothes
by Hank Zipzer

1. My Superman red boots
2. My Superman blue tights
3. My Superman red cape
4. My Donald Duck T-shirt
5. My other Donald Duck T-shirt
6. My pyjamas with the footballs on them
7. My Velcro trainers that light up when you run
8. My Mets baseball hat
9. My Batman underpants
10. Any trousers that don't have zips because I can't zip zips

My Superman red cape

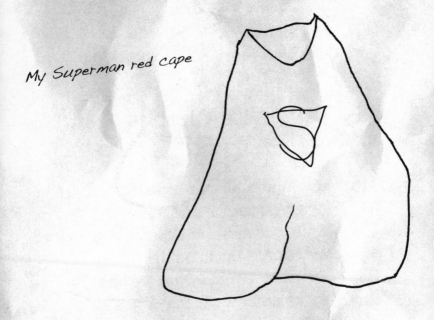

My Batman underpants

My Mets baseball cap

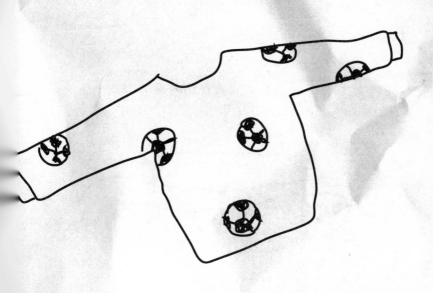

My pyjamas with the footballs on them

My First Mets Game

This is the ticket stub for my first Mets game ever. I went with Papa Pete and it was awesome. On the next page is a picture of the hot dog I ate at Shea Stadium. Papa Pete put onions on it by mistake so we had to scrape them off. If you look hard, you can still see a few onion chunks. Ick.

Onion chunks - barf!!!

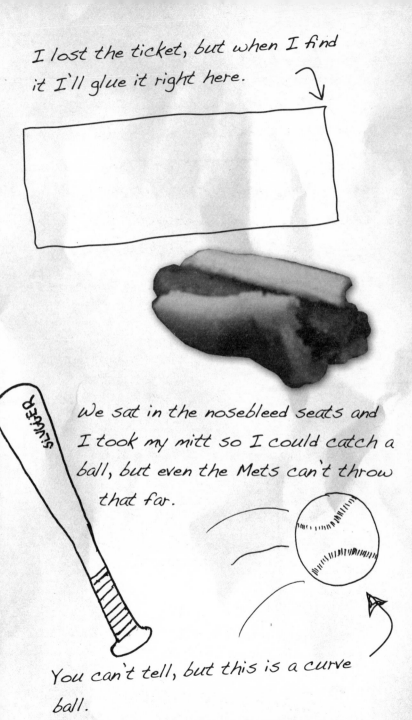

I lost the ticket, but when I find it I'll glue it right here.

We sat in the nosebleed seats and I took my mitt so I could catch a ball, but even the Mets can't throw that far.

SLUGGER

You can't tell, but this is a curve ball.

I Am Special Day

In first grade, we used to have "I Am Special" day. When it was your day, kids in the class got to say one thing they really liked about you. The teacher wrote their sentences down and you got to take the list home. This is my "I Am Special" list from Ms Yukelson's first-grade class.

Hank is special because he is my best friend.
– Ashley Wong

Hank is special because we have a secret handshake that only best best best friends have and I will never show anyone else as long as I live, I promise, Zip.
– Frankie Townsend

Hank is special because he shows a lot of teeth, on top and on bottom, when he smiles.
– Katie Sperling

Hank is special because he makes me laugh like a hyena.
– Salvatore Mendez

Hank is special because he has good manners and says excuse me when he burps on taco day.
– Heather Payne

Who says Hank is special? I think he's a big Zipperbutt. – Nick McKelty

Hank is special because he always has a tissue in his pocket when I need one for my bogeys.
– Luke Whitman

Hank is special because he only steps on my toes sometimes when we dance the "Hokey Pokey."
– Kim Paulson

Hank is special because he can touch his nose with his tongue. – Ryan Shimozato

Hank is special because he can whistle even when his lips are chapped. – Brandon Clarke

(By the way, I don't want to brag, but I really can whistle even when my lips are chapped. Try it, it's not easy.)

Ten Very Important Facts about Me

(Written by Hank Zipzer: age seven and almost a half written on 7 July when I was supposed to be having quiet time at Jones Beach on Long island.)

1. It's impossible for me to be quiet during quiet time. If I'm sitting, my leg bounces up and down. If I'm lying down, I keep flipping over.

2. My favourite meal for breakfast, lunch and dinner is Cheerios with chocolate milk. I call them Choc-ios.

3. My hair sticks up in the morning when I wake up. I look like a porcupine.

4. I don't like to get sand in my swimming trunks.

5. I don't know if the other word for sea is spelled oshun or otion or oschun. Anyway, it's big and blue and I don't know why.

6. I don't like to eat ice cream at the beach because the sun melts it faster than I can eat it and when it runs down my arm and I lick it, I get sand in my mouth.

7. I have 24 teeth and not one filling.

8. I am better at watching sports than playing them, except swimming. I'm good at the backstroke.

9. I DEFINITELY do not like to get water up my nose.

10. My middle toe is the longest toe on my left foot, but I keep it mostly hidden in a sock.

Ten Things That Are Hard for Me and I Wish They Weren't

(Written on 2 February by Hank Zipzer, who is in Ms Young's second-grade class.)

1. Reading
2. Remembering that I'm supposed to read
3. Spelling tests
4. Raising my hand in class before yelling out what I have to say

I'm going to stop for a few minutes because I have to go to the bathroom. I'll be right back.

5. Dribbling a basketball with one hand

Oops! Papa Pete just came in with a dill pickle for me. I'm going to get it.

This is a pickle juice drip.
Good thing you can't smell it.

Ummm ... where was I? Oh I remember,
number 6.

6. Finding my coat, and once I find it, remembering to take it with me
7. Colouring inside the lines or anywhere close to the lines
8. Adding and subtracting without using my fingers and toes
9. Keeping my notebook neat is easy. Knowing what to write in it is hard.
10. Getting my report and trying to explain to my dad why nothing but "gets along well with others" is good

Hooray! I've finished! I'm going to high-five myself.

Me and My Family

Cheerio as a Baby.
How Cute is he?

A piece of macaroni with a little
bit of cheese on it

A meatball, a real one, not the one
my mum makes out of tofu

A clean sock

P.U.!

A dirty sock

My versions of the letter H, which is the best letter in the alphabet because Hank starts with it

A Self Portrait
of Me
drawn by Me

(Wait a minute, I look better than this!)

Frankie's Magic Top Hat
(without the fake rabbit —
Oops! I gave away his secret).

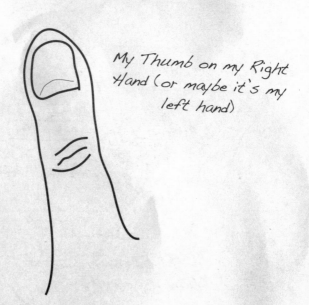

My Thumb on my Right
Hand (or maybe it's my
left hand)

A dolphin, which is
Ashley's favourite animal.
I know, I know it looks like a
shark. Give me a break I never said
I could draw.

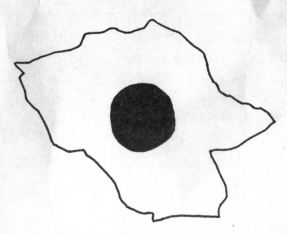

A sunny-side-up egg
before I break the yolk with my toast

How my swimming career tanked

When I was eight, I tried out for the swimming team at the YMCA, and guess what? I made it. I was even doing really well there for a while. Then my mum got this note in the post.

Dear Mrs Zipzer,

I am sorry to inform you that we had an incident today in the pool. Unfortunately, Hank had breakfast before practice, something I have warned my young swimmers never to do. As a result, he vomited while swimming the breaststroke. He left chunks of English muffins and what was apparently an omelette in the deep end of the pool.

As a result, Hank can no longer be a member of this team. But we thank him for his contribution up to this point.

Coach Robert Scudder

My First Note to the Tooth Fairy

Dear Mr or Mrs Tooth Fairy,

I have left my tooth under the pillow. I don't want any money for it. What I would like is for you to put my front tooth back in my mouth where it came from.

Thank you, Tooth Fairy.

Your friend,
Hank

Some more of my favourite
photos taken by me

A plate of slimy tofu that my mum tried
to get me to eat

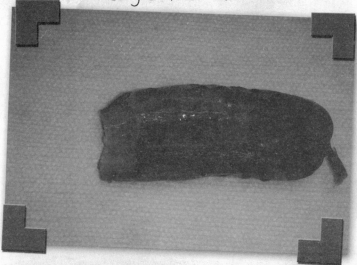

My favourite food — a dill pickle, just before it
disappeared into my stomach

This is a really pretty part of Central Park.

This is a really potty part of Central Park.
(Do not EVER ask me about the time I had to
use this.)

Cheerio's favourite pee stop

The day we tried to make eggrolls. We didn't know yo
weren't really supposed to roll the egg.

My desk (before I cleaned it)

My top desk drawer (after I cleaned it)
I know, I know, it looks the same.
That's what my dad always says.

A weird cat that sits in a window
I walk by on my way to school.
Once we stared each other down for
six minutes and forty seconds.
Until he got bored.

I lost these two photos,
so I've drawn them for you instead.

A banana with a funny face drawn on it.
Well, at least it's funny to me.

Harvey's pepperoni pizza, the best in the world

Two-Wheeled Certificate

When it came to learning how to ride a two-wheeled bike, you could say that I was a late bloomer. In fact, I bet I was the oldest kid in the tri-state area (that's New York, New Jersey and Connecticut) to learn how to ride a bike without training wheels. I finally did it in Greensboro, North Carolina, while we were on a family road trip to Florida. We were staying with my parents' friends and they had a boy and a girl the same age as Emily and me. They said, "Let's go and ride bikes" and I was too embarrassed to say I couldn't, so I just got on the bike and hoped for the best. To my complete surprise, I was able to balance for the first time, and from that day on, I could ride.

My mum made me this certificate.

This is to certify that

HANK ZIPZER

is a two-wheeled rider
and that from this day
forth, he no longer needs
stabilizers.

She was so proud of me.
Hey, I was proud of me!

My First Five Birthday Cakes from Age Zero to Ten

One Year Old – I just got mashed bananas because my mum wouldn't let me have sugar.

Two Years Old – A mashed string-bean cake with mashed apricot icing.

(I don't remember this cake, but they say I spat it out. I wonder why???)

Three Years Old – A chocolate cake with Superman on it.

(Papa Pete talked my mum into letting me have sugar on my birthday. Hooray for Papa Pete!)

Four Years Old – A yellow cake with Wonder Woman on it.

(My mum wanted me to know that women can be superheroes too.)

Five Years Old – No cake, but Trudi at Babka's Bakery made me a giant black-and-white cookie in the shape of a Panda bear.

(That was the year my mum discovered tofu and nothing in our kitchen would ever be the same again.)

List of My Teachers at School

Grade: Reception
Teacher: Ms McMurray
She was so nice. She gave us Graham crackers when we fell down and scraped our knees. And she didn't make me sleep during rest period.

Grade: 1st
Teacher: Ms Trager
She had a very scary face when she put on her mean look. I got into trouble for calling her Scary Face. She sure liked to give me Ds on my report.

Grade: 2nd
Teacher: Mrs Young
She would always eat chicken legs in class. Once, she borrowed my pencil and it was so greasy from her chicken leg fingers that I had to throw it away.

Grade: 3rd

Teacher: Mr Bass

He was sort of a cool guy. He loved "knock-knock" jokes, and he told me once that if schools gave out grades for telling "knock-knock" jokes, I would get straight As. That made me feel pretty good.

Grade: 4th

Teacher: Ms Adolf

If students got to give their teachers grades, I would give her straight As for being the World's Number One Sour Puss. I would pay a lot of money to see her laugh.

Grade: 5th

Teacher: Ms Adolf

Can you imagine getting Ms Adolf twice???? That is what I call Really Really Bad Luck!

My First-Grade Report

Report Card for Hank Zipzer
PS 87   Ms Trager's First-Grade Class

SUBJECT	Grade	Effort
Reading	D	A
Spelling	D	A
History	B	A
Science	D	A
Maths	D-	A

Teacher Comments: Hank is a very funny young man. However, he has got off to a slow start in first grade. His reading, spelling, science and maths skills need significant improvement. Hank tries very hard and always has his pencils sharpened and his school supplies ready. He plays well with others and is well liked by his peers.

As you can see, I didn't exactly get off to a rip snorting start in first grade. Luckily for me, I didn't really understand what a "D" was. Unluckily for me, my dad did!

My Second-Grade Report

Report Card for Hank Zipzer
PS 87   Ms Young's Second-Grade Class

SUBJECT	Grade	Effort
Reading	D	A
Spelling	D	A
History	B	A
Science	D	A
Maths	D-	A

Comments: Hank is a very likable and charming young man. However, his progress in second grade is rather disappointing. As we discussed at our parents' evening, his skills in all basic academic areas are well under par. Hank is accepted by his peers and always ready to entertain us with his excellent sense of humour.

I know, this report looks the same as my first grade one. No, you're not seeing double. This is basically what all my report cards look like. So I don't think I'm going to include any more report cards in this scrapbook.

Pictures I took of my school

It's called PS 87.

Here's the door.

Here's the window.
No duh.

These are pictures of the playground. Break is my favourite class.

I look at this sign every day on the way into school and on the way out of school. I like the way out better.

An Old Spelling Quiz

Mostly I don't save my tests and quizzes and stuff. If you look at this spelling quiz from third grade, I think you'll understand why. These are things a guy wants to forget!

Speling Quiz		
X	recieve	**Henry,** You need to study and take this again!
X	naahbor	
X	oshun	1/10 = F
X	teachar	
X	zeebra	
X	fish	
X	kurtin	
X	sox	
X	afrade	
X	tuff	

Here it is, folks, my valentine from Zoe.

Hank,
You Are My Hero!!!
With hugs from A
Secret Admirer
(Hint: I play the drums.)

About the Authors

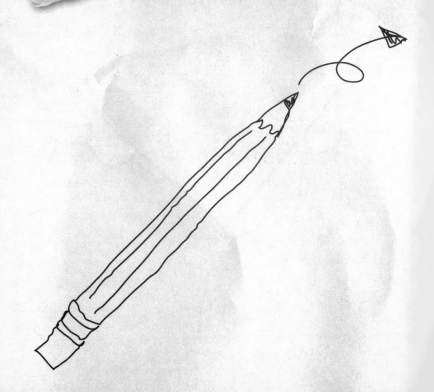

Hi Everyone,

Since Hank made a scrapbook for this book, we thought we'd make one, too. Well, it's not actually a whole scrapbook. It's more like a mini-scrapbook. We wanted to put in all kinds of cool scrapbook stuff, like shells that we found on the beach and dried flowers and the best pizza crust we've ever eaten, but our publishers wouldn't let us. They said it would get too messy.

Even though this is a little scrapbook, all the stuff in it is true. Those kids are really us. Those reports cards are really ours. And the pictures of those goofy grown-ups you see, yup, that's us, too.

We have to go now. After all, there are more Hank books to write. But thanks for flipping through these pages and saying hi. And we say a Big Hi right back at you.

Your pals,
Henry and Lin

Ten Things You should Know about Henry and Lin

1. They really love to write books together.

2. When they write, Lin sits in a beige leather chair and types very fast on her computer. Henry paces up and down on the rug in front of Lin's desk. They laugh a lot.

3. Lin has three sons named Theo, Ollie and Cole. Henry also has three children named Jed, Zoe and Max. In case you're not too good at maths, that makes six children.

4. Lin likes to eat tuna melts, chilli hot dogs and mint choc chip ice cream. Henry likes to eat pot roast with potato pancakes, pizza and a good chocolate bundt cake.

5. Henry and Lin have the same pet peeve, which is that they don't like people being mean to each other.

6. Henry's favourite pastimes are going to the theatre and fly-fishing for trout. Lin likes to make mosaics out of broken china and to cook, especially pot roast with potato pancakes.

7. They both enjoy reading letters from kids who think Hank is really funny.

8. Henry's birthday is 30 October, the day before Halloween. He loves answering the door when all the kids come in fancy dress. Lin's birthday is 2 February, which is also Groundhog Day. She loves to eat strawberry shortcake on her birthday.

9. Henry's favourite fruits are watermelon, bananas and honeydew melon. Lin loves all juicy red fruits and an occasional papaya.

10. Henry is married to Stacey whom he loves very much. Lin is married to Alan whom she loves most of the time, except when he beats her at Trivial Pursuit.

Here I am in Montana holding a brown trout.
I let him go back to his family right after
this picture was taken.

Here I am with my smart and wonderful wife,
Stacey.

The big Lab is named Linus. He is two years old.
The Labradoodle is Charlotte and she is six.

That's me
when I
was ten.
My teacher
was really
Miss Adolf,
maybe that's
why I'm not
smiling.

Henry's real-life stuff

Just like Hank, I had great spirit, if not great grades.

NAME __Henry Winkler__

In the development of these traits, the home shares responsibility with the school.

TRAINING IN PERSONALITY Desirable Traits	Oct. 31	Dec. 15	Jan. 31	Mar. 15	May 15	Jun. 30
1. Works and plays well with others	S	S	N	S		
2. Completes work	S	N	N	S		
3. Is generally careful	S	N	N	S		
4. Respects the rights of others	S	N	S	S		
5. Practices good health habits	S	S	S	S		
6. Speaks clearly	S	S	S	S		
7.						
8.						

Scholarship	Oct. 31	Dec. 15	Jan. 31	Mar. 15	May 15	Jun. 30
Reading	S	S	S	S		
Literature						
Composition	S	S	S	S		
Spelling	S	N	S	S		
Arithmetic	S	N	N	S		
Geography } social	S	S	S	S		
History and Civics } studies						
Penmanship	S	S	S	S		
Health Education	S	S	S	S		
Art	S	S	S	S		
Music	S	S	S	S		
Nature						
Sewing or Construction	S	S	S	S		

MEANING OF RATINGS

S—
A—
C—

So—Outstanding
S—Satisfactory
N—Needs Improvement
Nr—Not responding

is t

NEEDED IMPROVEMENT

First Period	Second Period	Third Period
	Spelling	math.
	arithmetic	spell.

Yes, it's true. Hank Zipzer is the story of my life.

Lin's real-life stuff

LIN

In high school, I wrote a column about our school for the local newspaper. And that's not a helmet I'm wearing ... that's my hair!

I won a writing award in high school, and I got to work as a reporter at the Los Angeles Times! It was so exciting.

This is my family on vacation in Hawaii. I'm on the end, and next to me are our sons Ollie, Cole and Theo, and on the other end, my husband, Alan. If you could smell this photo, it would smell like coconut suntan lotion.

This is me in my garden with my very naughty dog, Dexter. I'm the one without long black fur on my face.

I went to Mongolia to meet other children's book writers, but I met this grumpy eagle instead. We didn't get along.

This is me when I was eight months old. My teddy bear was named Rover, but I couldn't say that, so I called him Lovis.

We really have fun
writing these books
together.